TAMING HIS PRINCESS

Crossed Wires, book 1

MARI CARR

LEXXIE COUPER

Taming His Princess

Annie impetuously flies halfway around the world to visit a sexy cowboy she met online—only to find herself stranded in Sydney. Seems she and Dylan crossed wires, and he's on his way to New York.

His twin, Hunter, saves the day and whisks her back to the family cattle station. Hunter's as easy on the eyes as Dylan, and even easier to talk to. Annie might have flown to Oz to meet one brother, but sparks are flying with the other.

And while Hunter's not one to poach his brother's women, he can't keep his hands, lips, tongue, and other body parts off the sexy city girl.

When lust leads to attachment, where does that leave Annie and Hunter when her vacation comes to an end—or when Dylan finds out?

Annie: Mornin' sunshine!

Dylan: G'day, love. How're things in your neck of the woods this evening?

Annie: Long-ass day. Started with rain. Ended with rain. The middle bit was filled with my boss calling me Princess in a staff meeting. Grrrrr. I may end up killing him soon.

Dylan: Don't kill him. I'm too far away to bail you out.

Annie: LOL. Thanks for the offer, but Monet's already promised to have my back with the bail money.

Dylan: I think I like this Monet.

Annie: Yeah. She rocks. Actually, she might be the only thing rocking in my world these days.

Dylan: That doesn't sound good.

Annie: It's not. You ever been sick of your life, Dylan?

Dylan: Me? Sick of life? Nope. Sick of Hunter at times. The bloody bastard's been giving me a hard time about chatting with a woman in America again. I told him if he says another word, he's dead.

Annie: Careful. I'm too far away to bail you out. Snort! Sometimes I wish we lived closer.

Dylan: Me too, love. But let's be serious, a city girl wouldn't last a day in the Outback.

Annie: What? You must be joking. I'd last a hell of a lot longer on your little ranch than you would in my big city.

Dylan: Station, Annie. Station. We don't own ranches Down Under. Do you reckon you'd handle the snakes in the loo?

Annie: I deal with the rats in the sewers just fine.

Dylan: I'll accept your offer of rats in the sewers and give back crocs in the river and spiders on the toilet seat. How's that sound?

Annie: Deal.

Dylan: Two days. I'd give you two days before you were on a plane heading back to New York. Me, of course, well…I'd make one hell of a city boy. Blend in like I was born and bred there.

Annie: You wouldn't last a New York minute, tough guy.

Dylan: I tell you what. Let's see who outlasts the other. A Yank in the Outback or an Aussie in New York. Next week. Game?

Annie: Game on.

Dylan: Let me take a look at the flights online.

Annie: LMAO. Are we seriously doing this?

Dylan: I've never been more serious in my life. Okay. I'll see you in four days, city girl. This Saturday. Qantas. Sydney International. One p.m.

Chapter One

Annie Prince sank on to one of the hard plastic seats at Sydney Airport, giving in to exhaustion. She looked down at her very wet, now defunct iPhone—she vowed she'd never text on the toilet again—and decided this trip had been cursed from the word go.

In the past twenty-four hours she'd run the gamut of emotions—anger, frustration, annoyance, disappointment, excitement, happiness, sheer panic and now…nothing but numbness.

She studied the hubbub of the airport again. How the hell did she get here?

She'd roamed the International Arrivals area for nearly an hour before giving in to the realization he wasn't anywhere to be found. Dylan wasn't waiting for her.

When she'd replayed this scenario in her mind three thousand, four hundred and twenty-seven times—it had been a long-ass flight to Sydney—she'd always seen him standing in front of the crowd of families and friends waiting to welcome loved ones home. In her mind's eye, he'd been smiling widely, holding flowers, maybe even a balloon. She'd imagined he'd give a true cowboy woot when she stepped through the doors and every woman around them would watch with jealousy as he rushed over to pick her up, spin her around and kiss her.

Instead, she'd watched all her fellow travelers receive those warm welcomes while she stood completely alone, in a foreign country.

How the hell did I get here?

She closed her eyes wearily, thinking of that fateful night when she'd met Dylan online, the night that had set her on this misguided, insane path.

It was all Monet's fault.

"I CAN'T TELL you how much better I feel. Thanks for coming over, Monet."

"Wine cures everything," Monet announced. "You know that."

She and Monet had been neighbors in their high-rise Manhattan apartment building for nearly a year. They'd met on the elevator the day Monet moved in, and had clicked. Their friendship had flourished through numerous nights of drinking, broken hearts and, "oh my God, I just had awesome sex" chats.

"It cured my lousy day."

Monet topped up her wineglass. Annie winced when she noticed it was empty. Hadn't she just filled it up a few minutes ago?

"Damn." Monet squinted at the bottle. "That one went fast. Should we go for broke and make it a three-bottle night?"

Annie giggled. "Sure. Why not? My hangover is pretty much guaranteed at this point."

"So what's wrong?"

"My boss skipped over me for another big assignment, the paparazzi were out in full-force this afternoon and I dumped Joel."

Monet reared back. "That's a lot of shit for one day. Let's tackle this one at a time. Your boss is a prick. Why are you still working there?"

"Because it's one of the few magazines in New York my father doesn't own. You know how I feel about making it without his help."

"Pardon me, Annie, but you're not 'making it'. That asshole boss of yours is working against you."

Annie sighed. "I know."

"What's the deal with the paparazzi? Thought they'd become bored with you lately."

"That's actually connected to my breakup. Joel did a tell-all interview with People *magazine where he casually hinted there may be wedding bells in our future. What the fuck is that about? We've been dating five months and I have zero intention of locking myself in wedded hell with anybody right now. He knows that."*

Monet took a sip of wine and looked at her sympathetically. "You think he was trying to force your hand?"

Annie was too familiar with the Joels of the world. Unfortunately, she also sucked at recognizing them until after they'd screwed her—figuratively and literally. "He wants a piece of the Prince pie. I'm freaking done with men."

Monet rolled her eyes. "No, you're not. You enjoy sex too much."

"I'll hire a paid escort."

Monet laughed. "You're a romantic at heart and it's pretty obvious that's never going to change. If all your asshole exes haven't beaten that out of you, we can assume it's a character flaw that will stick."

"Great. So I'm destined for life as an old maid because every man in America wants my family's money a hell of a lot more than they want me."

"So broaden the search." Monet leaned over and grabbed her laptop from the coffee table.

"What are you doing?"

Monet didn't answer. Instead, she quickly tapped several keys on the computer then turned the screen around so Annie could see it.

"An online dating service? Be serious."

Monet raised an eyebrow. "I'm one-hundred-percent serious. I never joke around about getting laid. Let's assume that every man in the United States knows your family's name."

"Prince Incorporated has large holdings in Europe and Asia too," Annie pointed out. Her buzz was now full force. "So unless that service can find me a man on Mars, this is a waste of time."

Monet kept typing. "So we'll go extreme." Her eyes widened as her gaze landed on something on the screen. "Ooo la la. What do we have here?"

Annie tried to peer at the laptop, but Monet turned it away from her.

"What is it?"

Monet grinned. "What's your stance on a sexy Australian cowboy?"

"Jesus. They have those on there? Sign me up."

Monet giggled—and then she did just that.

ANNIE SIGHED and glanced around the airport once again. Sitting and sulking was accomplishing nothing. There were a thousand possible scenarios for why Dylan wasn't here. Maybe something had come up at the ranch.

Crap. *Station.* She'd never remember that.

Or maybe he was stuck in traffic, his car broken down. Maybe he'd gotten a nasty stomach flu. She'd walked by a customer service desk at least a dozen times during her trips around the terminal searching for her cowboy. She'd ask them to do an all-call over the intercom. She needed to determine Dylan truly wasn't here before she tried to figure out her next move.

As she waited in line to speak to the representative, she remembered the morning after her impulsive, drunken decision to join the world of international online dating.

She'd woken up bleary-eyed, with a pounding headache, and had decided to call in sick to work. Annie had never taken a sick day, but her boss's determination to treat her like a nonentity and her queasy stomach made the choice to remain home an easy one.

SHE WALKED *toward the kitchen for a handful of saltines, stopping to power up her laptop on the way. When she returned to her desk, she discovered an email from someone she didn't know. Dylan Sullivan. Her hand hovered over the button that would send Mr. Sullivan straight to the trash, but something stopped her. Some niggling memory from the previous night.*

She and Monet had drunk way too much and stayed up far too late. Monet had consoled her over work and Joel.

Oh fuck! The online dating gag. Monet had signed her up and then…

Some Aussie cowboy had expressed interest. Monet had talked her into sharing her personal information.

Annie rubbed her aching head. How could she have been so stupid? If the tabloids caught wind of the "practical Prince sister" soliciting for dates online, they'd be ruthless. She might as well give up any hope of avoiding the limelight. Maybe she should just pack it in and join her ditzy sisters' ridiculous reality show, Life with the Princesses. *It's not like she'd ever be taken seriously after this little tidbit leaked out.*

Her hand hovered over the mouse, and then she quickly clicked to open the email. She'd gone this far. She might as well see what she was risking her reputation for. She read Dylan's message.

His email was nice, well written and humorous. It also seemed pretty clear he had no idea who Annie Prince was.

Feeling like she'd dodged a bullet, Annie responded, explaining nicely that she'd been tipsy when her friend talked her into signing up for the service. She let him down as gently as she could, turned off the computer and crawled back into bed with a couple of aspirin and a tall glass of ice water.

When she awoke later that afternoon, she was surprised to find a very funny response from her would-be Aussie suitor. Dylan had taken her rejection with good grace and he'd even sent her a list of ingredients for the Sullivan family hangover cure. Against her better judgment, Annie tried the hangover recipe, which worked, and then wrote Dylan again, thanking him.

AFTER THAT, they'd fallen into a pattern of emailing every day. If anyone asked her to list her three closest friends at the moment, Dylan would be included on the list. For the past few months, they'd talked about anything and everything. She'd even taken a huge leap of faith and told Dylan about her family and their money. Monet had been correct. Australians—at least those in Dylan's neck of the woods—didn't have a clue who the Prince family was.

"May I help you, miss?"

Annie glanced up and discovered she was next in line. "Yes. I was hoping you could page someone for me. My friend was supposed to pick me up about an hour ago, but I can't find him."

The airport employee nodded and gave her what looked like a pitying smile. "Of course. What's your friend's name?"

"Dylan Sullivan."

"I'll page him right away. Should I have him meet you here?"

Annie murmured a quiet "yes, thanks," then stepped away from the desk to wait as Dylan's name was broadcast throughout the airport.

Please God, let him hear it. Let him be here.

Not only was her sex life depending on him being the

good guy she believed him to be—she'd foolishly hitched the success of her career to Dylan's wagon as well.

Miraculously, she'd managed to convince her editor, Mr. Lennon, to let her write a four-part series for the magazine about life on an Australian cattle station. It was the only way she'd managed to swing the trip across the ocean and the time away from work on such short notice. He'd only agreed because *his* boss saw the picture of Dylan that she'd attached to the proposal. Apparently the editor-in-chief had a thing for Aussie cowboys too. She'd demanded Lennon give Annie the assignment, and he'd begrudgingly complied.

There was no way she could go home without the articles and expect to keep her lousy job.

"Come on, Dylan," she muttered. "Where the hell are you?"

***

HUNTER RAN his finger down the pretty blonde's arm, enjoying the flirting and easy banter. He'd hit the bar after seeing his idiot brother off at his gate. They'd flown the station helicopter to Sydney, leaving so early this morning it had still been dark. Hunter had a couple of hours to kill while he waited for the flight mechanic to refuel the chopper and clear him for takeoff.

"So you live on a cattle station?" the blonde asked. He'd forgotten her name the second she'd said it. One of these days he was going to have to learn to pay attention to details like that.

"Yep. Farpoint Creek. My family's owned it forever. Established it back in the 1800s."

The woman feigned interest, but Hunter could see the disdain in her eyes. She was clearly a city girl and the idea of living out whoop whoop in the Outback was less than appealing to her. Lucky for both of them, he wasn't considering taking this game of slap and tickle out of the airport.

She leaned closer, *accidentally* brushing the side of his arm with her breast. They'd started their flirting at different tables. Then he'd joined her. After a few minutes of sexual innuendoes, he'd given up his seat across the table and moved over to share her side of the booth.

"You know, I'm a member of the Qantas Club."

"Is that right?" he asked.

"I was actually thinking of heading over there and freshening up before my flight. They have showers in the lounge."

"Showers, eh? Bit bloody fancy."

She dragged her hand along his leg, starting at his knee and working her way up. He liked a woman who knew what she wanted and wasn't afraid to grab it. His dick twitched when her hand crept closer.

"Wish I had someone to wash my back," she purred.

He started to offer his sudsy services, but something on the PA caught his attention. "What did she say?"

"What did *who* say?"

The PA announcement was repeated. *Dylan Sullivan, please meet your party at the customer service desk located at terminal one.*

What the hell? Dylan wasn't here. At least, he bloody well shouldn't be.

Hunter reluctantly pushed the woman away while silently cursing his brother. "Sorry, love, but I gotta go do something." Dylan would pay dearly for costing him a shower with this beauty in the high flyer's club. He retrieved his hat from the table and put it back on his head.

"You're leaving?"

Hunter nodded regretfully. "Yeah. Afraid it can't be

helped." He threw enough cash on the table to cover both of their drinks and a generous tip for the waitress. "Sorry."

He walked toward terminal one, trying to figure out why Dylan wasn't jetting away from Sydney, getting closer to making one of the dumbest mistakes of his life. He'd loaded his brother on a plane headed for New York over an hour ago.

Hunter had spent most of their morning trek to Sydney trying to convince Dylan that taking off halfway around the world to hook up with some broad he'd met on one of those stupid online dating services made him look pretty desperate.

He'd also pointed out that precious little could come of this trip, besides getting a piece of New York tail. Dylan lived and worked on Farpoint Creek cattle station. In Australia. Trying to hook up with some American chick wasn't exactly practical.

Dylan, ever the romantic idiot, seemed to think Annie had the potential to be his soul mate. Jesus, his brother had actually used those words—*soul mate*—and was supposed to be headed to New York to prove that asinine fact.

Had Dylan missed his plane? Hunter couldn't figure out how. They'd made it to the departure gate in plenty of time. And if so, why would he page *himself* rather than ask the customer service rep to page Hunter? Maybe Dylan had given his own name as well and the lady had fucked it up.

He glanced at the crowd standing around the service desk as he walked toward the terminal. He and Dylan weren't lacking in the height department. If his dickhead brother was around, he sure as hell wasn't standing up; he'd tower over these people. Add the fact he and Dylan hardly ever took off their bloody hats and Hunter should be able to spot him a mile away.

He started to get in line at the desk to ask who'd paged Dylan when a woman walked up to him.

"You're here!" she said.

Hunter tried to place the woman's face. She looked vaguely familiar. "I am?" His mother claimed he'd been cursed with a sarcastic streak as wide as Farpoint since the day he was born. While his mum found it annoying, Hunter had never found a good reason to curb that personality trait.

The pretty woman smiled. "I was starting to worry."

Before he could tell her she had the wrong bloke and should go ahead and hang on to her anxiety, she took a step closer and threw her arms around him.

The hard-on Hunter had managed to batten down as he'd walked away from his potential shower partner reemerged when her firm breasts brushed against his chest. Bloody hell. Who knew the airport was such a great place to pick up women? He might have to fly to Sydney International more often.

Never one to pass up an opportunity, he accepted the embrace, loosely wrapping his arms around her back. The lovely lady was just the right height for him and had some sexy curves. He liked a woman with meat on her bones.

She pulled away slightly and he started to release her, but she kept her arms wrapped around him and upped the ante, kissing him.

It started as a sweet, friendly kiss, but Hunter wasn't having any of that shit. She smelled and tasted too good. He grasped her soft face and held her close. He turned his head and deepened the kiss, pressing her lips open so he could get an even better taste. He was thrilled when her tongue met his halfway. Jesus. This chick could kiss.

The flash of a camera distracted him and he felt the woman stiffen slightly. He ignored both, pressing his lips more firmly against hers. She relaxed—then another camera flashed. And another.

He thought he heard the woman mutter the word "fuck" as she stepped away.

"We need to get out of here," she said.

With some distance between them, Hunter's brain reengaged. It was clear she had the wrong guy, but it was going to be awkward to admit that, given the liberties he'd taken with her mouth.

"Listen, love—" he began.

She ignored him. Bending over, she retrieved her suitcases. Handing one to him, she briskly walked away from the service desk. He dragged her bag and tried to keep up.

"Where's your car?" she asked.

"Don't have one."

That admission stalled her for a moment. "Dylan, the paparazzi have spotted me. We've gotta get out of here."

Two words resonated in his brain. "Dylan" and "paparazzi".

Who the bloody hell *was* this woman?

More flashes. Hunter glanced over his shoulder and saw three men with cameras following them. People turned to stare, curiously trying to determine which famous person was walking through Sydney airport.

Hunter grabbed her hand. "Here, this way."

He led her toward the terminal where his helicopter awaited. He glanced at the time as they passed under a clock. The thing should be fueled up and ready by now. The cameramen continued to dog their steps. There were nearly a dozen people trailing them now as cameras continued to flash. He showed his ID at the terminal, they were ushered through a doorway and, at last, the paparazzi were shut out.

"Who the hell *are* you?" he asked as they paused in the small hallway that led to the tarmac and his helicopter.

She pulled her hand from his grip and frowned, clearly unhappy about his question. "I told you about my family, Dylan. I warned you this could happen."

"Love, you didn't warn me about a damn thing. Why don't we start at the beginning? I'm *Hunter* Sullivan." He stressed his first name. "Now, who are you?"

The woman paled slightly. Hunter was impressed when she recovered quickly. She looked like she'd been run through the wringer but she clearly wasn't beaten yet.

"You're Dylan's brother."

He nodded. "We're twins. Obviously."

Annie studied his face. "Identical."

He didn't respond. She clearly knew his brother's face well enough to know there wasn't much to distinguish one from the other. Apart from the fact Dylan shaved less than him, they were mirror images. "And now that we've determined who I am, who are—"

"Why did you kiss me back there?"

Shit. Hunter was hoping she'd forget that little tidbit. The answer was simple—pure, instant animal attraction. He'd been worked up and horny as shit after his encounter with the blonde in the bar.

What he told *her* was different, and he tried not to wince at his own cocky, arrogant tone. "When a pretty broad throws herself at me, I'm not likely to refuse."

Her eyes narrowed. "I didn't *throw myself* at you. If you were any sort of gentleman, you would have told me who you were right away."

"Kind of hard to talk when someone's got their tongue in your mouth."

"You put your tongue in my mouth first."

Hunter grinned and took a step closer, looking at her

lips once more. He raised his eyebrows as if to say he'd do it again if given the chance.

She glanced at the door they'd just walked through. Hunter could read the indecisiveness on her face. He wondered if she'd subject herself to another dash through the airport with the paparazzi hot on her heels or if she'd tough it out with him. Given his current behavior, he'd choose the cameramen if he was her. He was being a right bloody arsehole.

"Listen, maybe if you told me who you were, I could help you get where you need to be. You're obviously not from here. American, right?" But as soon as he asked the question, a horrifying reality crashed down on his head. "*Annie?*"

The woman nodded.

"You're *Dylan's* Annie? From New York?" The fact she was here wasn't sinking into his thick skull as quickly as it should.

"Yes. Is he okay? Is there a reason why he sent you to pick me up? He's not ill, is he?"

Hunter shook his head. "No. He's not sick. He's on his way to see *you*." Hunter glanced at his watch. "His plane will land at JFK in about eighteen hours."

"I don't understand."

"Neither do I. I'd say you two crossed wires somewhere. Ordinarily I'd suggest we head to the terminal, hit a bar and make a plan about where to go from here, but I suspect you don't want to go back there with all those cameramen breathing down your neck."

Annie shook her head.

"Is there anyone you can call?"

She repeated the headshake. "I dropped my phone in the toilet when I was texting Dylan to find out where he was. It's officially dead."

Hunter bit the inside of his cheek to keep from laughing. The poor woman was having a rough day.

"Is there somewhere more private we can hide out?" she asked. "Until I figure out what I'm supposed to do now."

Hunter pointed down the corridor. "I guess we could sit in the chopper."

"Chopper?"

He grasped the handles on both her suitcases and began dragging them as he walked toward the runway. He was pleased when Annie followed rather than run in the opposite direction.

"Dylan and I came to the airport in a helicopter."

Annie gave him a funny look. "You have a thing against cars?"

"You have any idea how big Australia is? We live damn near in the middle of it, love. We could either fly the chopper to the airport in four or five hours or drive to Sydney in just under a dozen. I can't afford to be away from work for so long, so it was a pretty easy decision. I flew Dylan here early this morning and intend to fly home later today."

"This can't be happening," Annie muttered behind him. "How could this all get so fucked up?"

Hunter picked up the bags and carried them down the stairs to the tarmac, where his chopper sat waiting.

A flight mechanic approached. "You've got a full tank, Mr. Sullivan, and I gave everything a quick inspection. It's ready to roll. Just radio the air traffic control room when you're ready for takeoff."

"Thanks, mate. Will do."

Hunter threw her luggage in the back. Annie paused when he opened the passenger door of the helicopter for her. "Who flies this?"

"I do."

"Jesus. Are you serious?"

Hunter suppressed a grin. Her American accent was cute. "Yes, Annie. I'm a fully qualified helicopter pilot. Not that you need to worry. We're just hiding out in here, right?"

Annie bit her lip as she looked up at the propellers nervously. Rather than reply, she tried to climb into the passenger seat. The devil prodded him forward and he gave her a boost, using her arse for leverage. It was firm, tight. It took all this strength not to give it a good squeeze.

She startled when he placed his hands on her rear end, but accepted the momentum he provided to claim her seat. "Thanks." Her slightly narrowed eyes and sardonic tone almost made him laugh.

"My pleasure." He crossed in front of the chopper and took his place behind the controls. "So I guess we need to figure out how you ended up *here* when Dylan said he was going *there*."

"He didn't say he was going to New York. We were chatting on IM and he said something like 'put your money where your mouth is'. Then he said Qantas, Sydney Airport, November twentieth, and gave me a time. I booked the flight, even though the arrival time he listed was a bit off, but I figured that's because airlines are constantly changing their schedules."

Hunter frowned. "I was there when he sent that stupid — *Ahem*." He cleared his throat uncomfortably. "I saw him send you the flight details—*his* flight details—in an email about an hour after that. He forwarded you the information from the airline."

Annie looked around the helicopter and he wondered what she was thinking. "I never got that email."

"Well, he sent it." Hunter didn't want to mention that

satellite reception on Farpoint Creek was sketchy at best. There was a very good chance Dylan's email was still bouncing around somewhere in space.

Annie sighed. "I swear to you I never got it. I just said 'challenge accepted' or 'game on' or something in our chat."

He nodded. "Yeah, Dylan took that to mean you were excited about his visit. Bloody dickhead."

"But I meant I was coming *here*. I thought he'd invited me to Australia."

"Well, I don't mean to criticize, love, but what woman accepts an invitation to visit a bloke she's never met in a foreign country and only gives herself four days to prepare? Didn't your family and friends try to talk you out of this?"

Annie's shoulders straightened and he could see she was pissed off. "I *know* Dylan."

He rolled his eyes. "A few emails and IMs and—"

"We've been corresponding for months. Plus we've Skyped and talked on the phone and exchanged pictures. I feel like I *do* know him."

"And I suppose from that kiss you gave me back in the terminal, you didn't intend for this to be just a friendly visit."

She bit her lip again. Hunter wished he didn't find the gesture so cute. "That's none of your business."

He let her off the hook. Her blush answered his question just fine. "What's the deal with the paparazzi? You an actress or something?"

"Dylan didn't tell you about my family?"

Hunter shook his head. "Nope. Dylan didn't share much about you at all. Showed me a photo of you a few weeks ago. Besides that and the fact you don't read your emails carefully, I don't know a thing about you." Hunter didn't mention the soul mate comment.

"I'm a journalist. I work for a magazine in New York."

"Didn't realize journalists were so popular in the States."

She flashed him a dirty look. "It's not my job that interests the press, it's my name. I'm Annie Prince."

He shook his head. "I'm still not following you."

"Prince Incorporated?"

Hunter recognized that name even less. "Nope. Haven't got a bloody clue what you're talking about."

"I guess Monet was right. She said there had to be somewhere on the planet where I could live incognito. Go Australia." She raised one fist in a cheer for his country.

"I don't know who this Monet is, but that's not exactly true. You're in Sydney and there are cameramen following you."

She blew out a long, frustrated breath. "Yeah. My family owns and operates a huge conglomeration of newspapers, magazines, hotels and other properties. Our net worth is in the billions. For some insane reason, this makes us interesting to people. Not to mention the fact my dad is a bit of a glory hound, constantly doing stuff to draw attention to himself. My two sisters have followed in his footsteps and now star on the most inane, idiotic reality series ever to air on television. And I suppose everyone expects me to be the same, to want the same spotlight cast on my life."

"But you don't?"

"*God* no. Did you see me pose for photos? Your ranch in the middle of the desert actually sounds like paradise."

Hunter scoffed. "I think you're the first woman, besides my mother, to ever feel that way. And it's not a ranch. It's a station."

Annie ignored his correction. Maybe she was used to it. He'd heard Dylan tell her a time or two when he'd accidentally eavesdropped on their chats. She let out a wobbly sigh. "What the hell am I going to do now?"

Hunter studied her desolate face and was sorry Dylan *hadn't* invited her for a visit. The idea of Annie spending a week or two on their family's cattle station was very appealing.

Then he recalled Dylan's comment. *She could be my soul mate.* He couldn't poach on his brother's girl.

"Seems to me your answer's simple. Go back inside and catch the next flight out of Sydney. Chances are it won't leave until tomorrow, so you could book a hotel in the city and take in a couple of the sights. No reason the trip has to be a total waste. You'll only be a day or so behind Dylan. Once you get back, the two of you can take New York by storm. No harm, no foul."

Annie didn't respond for several moments. Finally she released another sigh, this one less wobbly. "I can't go back to New York right away."

Hunter frowned. "Why not? If you're worried about those wankers with the cameras, I can talk to security, get you an escort."

She shook her head. "It's not that. I'm here for work as well. On an assignment for the magazine. It was the only way I could miss two weeks of work. I haven't been there long enough to build up any real vacation time."

"What's your assignment?"

"I'm writing a four-part series about life on a cattle station. And I'm supposed to interview a real live Aussie cowboy."

She looked at him hopefully—and he knew he was in trouble.

"I'm a stockman, Annie. We're called stockmen over

here, or grazier, if we're being more formal. Which we're not."

"Oh. Okay. Then I need to shadow a stockman."

"Me?"

She lifted one shoulder as if to ask *why not*. "I'd intended to interview Dylan, but he's not here and likely won't be for a while. The first piece is due in three days and once I start, I sort of need to stick with the same cow…er, stockman."

She really expected him to take her back to the cattle station? Let her follow him around for two weeks watching him work? How was he supposed to keep his hands off her if she was under his roof and his bloody brother was half a world away?

Dylan better get his arse back Down Under, and quick.

Otherwise, this was not going to end well.

Chapter Two

"You should have told me you were afraid of flying, love. This isn't a short flight."

Annie slowly lifted her eyelids and forced herself to take a steadying breath. Her eyes had been pressed firmly closed for at least half an hour. She wasn't used to being able to see so much while in the air. Typically she opted for an aisle seat on airplanes, careful to keep her eyes glued to the back of the seat in front of her. That way she could pretend she was on the ground instead of thousands of feet above. Between that and the drowsiness caused by the Dramamine she'd taken, she'd managed to remain somewhat calm during the long flight to Oz.

Unfortunately, the large windows in the helicopter didn't afford her the luxury of forgetting where she was.

"I was afraid you'd make fun of me."

From her peripheral vision, she could see him staring at her. She wanted to yell at him to keep his eyes on the road or the air or whatever.

"I don't find other people's fears funny. I hate snakes. *Hate* them. Dylan used to catch 'em and stick 'em in my bed all the time when we were kids. Do you think that's funny?"

She shook her head. "No, but maybe that's because I'm afraid of *them* too."

He shook his head and snorted. "So who's the arsehole who's been giving you shit about your flying issues? Want me to beat him up?"

"It's more like three arrrs-holes," she mimicked. "Though I don't suppose I should use that word when speaking of my dad and sisters."

Hunter's scowl grew. "Your family makes fun of you because you're afraid of flying?"

"Maybe that's the wrong expression. They just seem to find humor in my fear of flying because our father owns a private jet, and he would prefer to take it to the grocery store rather than drive if given the choice. My entire family is made up of jetsetters. And then you have me. The daughter who's a bit out of place. Odd guy out. As always."

He continued to look at her closely. "You don't seem that odd to me. Although given the fact you're lost in Oz at the moment, I'd agree with the misplaced part."

"Would you mind watching where you're going? I really can't concentrate on what you're saying when you're looking at *me* instead of out there." She waved her hand toward the front window, pointing at the sky before them.

Hunter chuckled. "Sorry, love. Didn't mean to scare you."

She sucked in another ragged breath, relieved when he faced forward once more.

"I'm sorry. I didn't mean to snap at you."

Hunter fiddled with a button near the controls. "Is that what that was? Snapping? Hell, love, spend a few days with my mum and you'll learn how to *really* give a man a piece of your mind."

Dylan had mentioned they lived on Farpoint Creek with their mother. Now Annie found herself a new thing to worry about. What if Mrs. Sullivan didn't like her? Obviously the family wasn't expecting company for two weeks. Not only was she imposing on Dylan's brother, she was inflicting herself on his mother as well.

Hunter distracted her when he asked, "Why were you on a Qantas flight if your dad owns a jet? Wouldn't he let you borrow it?"

They were getting into slightly more personal territory. Annie had lived most of her life on guard, holding her cards close to her chest, not giving too many people a peek. Monet knew most of her issues regarding her family and she'd also confided a few things to Dylan. She'd stressed her desire that he not tell anyone about the secrets she'd divulged and, given Hunter's obliviousness regarding her life, she'd been right to trust Dylan. He hadn't betrayed her, not even to his own family.

"I try not to take advantage of my father's wealth." While that statement was the truth, it was also a lie in terms of this trip. She hadn't used the jet because she hadn't told her family she was leaving the country.

"Sort of cutting off your nose to spite your face, wouldn't you say? If my dad had billions, I think I'd find it hard not to indulge every once in a while."

Annie rolled her eyes. "I'm not saying I'm not totally spoiled. I grew up with the proverbial silver spoon in my mouth. I went to the best private schools in the States. Spent my summers on yachts and vacationing in some of the most beautiful places in the world. All my clothes had designer labels dangling from them and my primary mode of transportation was a limousine."

"I'm struggling to find a problem in all that, love."

She leaned her head against the headrest. "All of that comes with a cost. The paparazzi trail me everywhere—practically night and day—thinking my life is lived for *their* entertainment. They tend to be cruel on bad hair days or if I wear something they deem to be in poor taste. I can't go to the grocery store without makeup or they start rumors that I'm sick or suffering from depression or a broken heart or something stupid like that. Usually the truth is I was too lazy to shower and get all dolled up just to run out for a lousy gallon of milk."

"Yeah, that would get old quick."

Annie remembered how Hunter had gone in to protector mode at the airport. He'd kept a cool head and gotten them away from the growing pack of rabid cameramen. "You were really great back there, by the way. I don't think I said thank you for getting me away from those damn flashing lights. I hate cameras almost as much as flying."

Hunter gave her a crooked grin. "No worries."

He was easy to talk to, like his brother. She wasn't sure what the difference was between the Sullivan men and all the other guys she'd ever dated, but there was definitely something that set them apart. Maybe it was that they didn't look at her and see dollar signs. More than that, they both seemed genuinely interested in her as a person. It was unique and very, *very* attractive.

She closed her eyes once more, but not out of fear as much as an attempt to relax. It has been a long journey and they still had a ways to go. She felt like she'd been in the air for days.

They continued chatting for a while. The helicopter was warm and the sound of the propellers created a soothing rhythm in the small space and, before she knew it,

Annie found herself telling Hunter things she'd never told anyone, not even Monet or Dylan. She spoke of her childhood friends, summer camp and raucous college parties.

"Uni girl, eh? Dylan and I sort of skipped that part in our education and went straight to work on the station."

"That's a shame. You missed some awesome fraternity parties."

He shook his head. "You've obviously never gotten drunk by the campfire with a bunch of rowdy jackaroos after long weeks of mustering."

"Our lives seem to be as different as sardines and caviar. I remember the night I graduated magna cum laude at college—"

"Magner cum who?" he interjected.

Annie giggled softly. "I graduated with honors. Top of the class. Like how I managed to work that into the conversation?" she joked.

Hunter gave her a solemn nod, those his eyes twinkled with mirth. "Very smooth. Only took you about an hour. Congrats on being a smart arse."

She narrowed her eyes, pretending to be insulted, though she suspected her grin was giving away how much fun she was having. "Anyway, to recognize my undisputable brilliance, my father threw a way-over-the-top party to celebrate. There were hundreds of people in attendance, most of them I didn't even know. We were in the giant ballroom of a grand hotel Dad had recently purchased. He pulled me aside, said he had a gift for me. He handed me a contract that said *The New York Bulletin* was mine."

Hunter frowned and she was reminded they really *did* live in two different worlds. "*Bulletin?*"

"It's a major newspaper in the city. My dad owns it."

"Don't you mean *you* own it?"

She shook her head. "I turned it down. A light went on

in my head that night. I'd worked my ass off all through high school and college, earning good grades because I wanted to make him proud of me. I chose journalism because that was my dad's major. He'd started his career as a reporter at the *Bulletin*, working his way up through the ranks until he was the owner of that and at least twenty other media—newspapers, magazines, publishing houses, cable channels. From there he branched out into real estate —rentals, office buildings, hotels."

Hunter took off his hat and tossed it on the backseat. He ran his hand through his light brown hair. Now that she studied him, she could see slight differences between him and his brother. Hunter's hair looked a wee bit longer than Dylan's and even though he was laughing with her, there was a seriousness around his eyes that she'd never noticed in his more easygoing brother.

His jaw was covered with stubble that indicated he hadn't bothered to shave before leaving the house this morning, but she suspected that wasn't normal. Dylan liked to joke about Hunter's fastidious morning routine, which apparently always included shaving. She ached to reach out and rub her hand along the rough shadow. Every time he smiled at her, it framed some of the sexiest dimples she'd ever seen.

Annie watched him with hooded eyes, wishing he wasn't so freaking gorgeous. With or without the hat, he took her breath way.

"Don't you think your father's gift was sort of special?" Hunter asked. "If the *Bulletin* was where he started, it had to have some sentimental value to him."

"Maybe. But that wasn't the point of all my hard work, was it? I didn't want him handing me my future on a silver platter. I wanted to earn it, the same way he did."

"I can understand that."

"Yeah, well, my dad didn't. Apparently he'd invited a ton of press to the party and he'd planned some grand announcement about me following in his footsteps. My refusal to accept the gift screwed up his moment in the sun."

Hunter looked at her once more, but this time she didn't complain about his lack of attention on where they were going. Instead she met his gaze, touched by the compassion she found in his deep-green eyes.

"My dad died of a massive heart attack when Dylan and I were fourteen. We had to find our footing fast. Luckily we had Mum. She's a tough bloody bugger and a force to be reckoned with. She guided us, taught us how to run Farpoint, but she also let us find our own way with it, let us make it our own. She never told us we had to do things a certain way because that's how Dad did it."

"Your mom sounds awesome."

The cutest crinkles appeared by Hunter's eyes. When he smiled, his whole face expressed happiness. "She's all right. I guess what I'm saying is no one ever told me who to be or how to live my life. If I fuck up, the blame's all mine, but at least I had the chance to make the mistake in the first place."

He did understand. Completely.

"That's what I want, to have the chance to succeed or fail. My dad doesn't agree. He says he's worked hard all his life so I won't have to."

"I can understand wanting to take care of your kids, but you're an adult now. I mean at, what, twenty-three, twenty-four, you're ready to stand on your own two feet."

He was fishing for her age, so she gave it to him. "I'm twenty-eight."

"Ah, only a couple years behind me and Dylan. So what happened after you turned down the gift?"

"My dad wasn't happy about it, but eventually he accepted my decision. Unfortunately, I didn't understand exactly how hard it was going to be to cut ties to my family's name. I managed to land a job at a small, independent magazine my dad doesn't own, but now my boss, Mr. Lennon, seems to think I'm just slumming it. I sort of suspect the editor-in-chief pressured him to hire me as a favor to my dad or maybe as a feather in her cap, but I have no proof of that. Mr. Lennon has zero expectation that I'll stick it out because, as he says, 'It's not like I need the money.'"

"Wow, what a wanker."

"Plus, I sort of failed at the living-on-my-own thing too. I found an apartment in Brooklyn I could afford on my salary, but it didn't have the best security and tabloid reporters broke in a few times and stole some personal stuff. The third time, I came home in the midst of the robbery. The guy freaked out about being caught red-handed. He shoved me down trying to get away and I ended up with a concussion when my head hit an end table."

Hunter's expression was thunderous. "Bloody hell! Hope they caught the fucker."

Annie nodded. "They did, but my dad put his foot down after that and insisted I move somewhere safer."

"Good for him."

Annie's heart warmed at how intently he listened. She genuinely liked Hunter Sullivan. He reminded her a bit of his brother, but she sensed there were some definite differences in their personalities too. Hunter's sense of humor seemed slower to come and more sarcastic, where Dylan was clearly a fun-loving guy who was quick to laugh and joke. Hunter also had a bit of a bad-boy edge Annie had never seen in Dylan. His easy acceptance of a kiss from a strange woman in the airport and the way he'd turned her friendly buss into pure lip sex proclaimed that loud and clear.

"Now I live in a high-rise Manhattan apartment with top-notch security that my dad pays for. It makes it hard for my colleagues and Mr. Lennon to accept my assertions that I want to be self-sufficient."

"The old *damned if you do, damned if you don't* scenario, eh?"

"Yeah. Something like that." She yawned. The helicopter was surprisingly comfortable. She felt like she was in a cozy cocoon. Hunter had offered her a blanket prior to takeoff.

"Here." Hunter reached behind his seat for a pillow. "Close your eyes. You've already had a long trip and we've got more than a few kilometers to go before we get to Farpoint. Try to get some sleep."

"I wanted to keep you company, so you don't get tired." Even as she spoke, her head was sinking into his proffered pillow.

"I'd planned to make this return trip alone, remember? Besides, I had a good night's sleep in my own bed last night. I'm fine."

She'd barely scraped a few hours of restless sleep on the plane. She felt like she should resist the temptation. God knew if she weren't so fatigued she'd never be able to fall asleep in the helicopter. Exhaustion was winning over fear.

She closed her eyes and the last thing she heard was Hunter saying, "Sweet dreams."

WHEN SHE WOKE up much later, it was dark. "What time is it?"

"G'day, love. I was about to check your pulse to make sure you were still breathing. It's nearly nine."

"How long did I sleep?"

"About three hours. I think you might have managed a bit more, but my fiddling with the controls probably woke you up. I'm getting ready to land."

"Now? We're here? At Farpoint?" Annie gripped the door handle and tried to calm her suddenly racing heart. She wished she'd managed to remain unconscious through this part. Takeoffs and landings were always the worst for her.

"Yep. Home sweet home. I'm sorry we're not landing in the daytime. I would have woken you earlier so you could see the spread. Now it's just a whole lotta black and the homestead in the middle of it. The station's fairly large; in addition to the helicopter pad, we have a landing strip. A plane arrives once a week to deliver mail and supplies. If you want, I'll take you up again in a couple days and let you get a feel for the land."

The idea of spending any more time in the air was as appealing as a trip to the gynecologist, but she held her peace. Hunter appeared to be concentrating on bringing the chopper down. If she weren't already so terrified, her anxiety would have exploded at the idea of landing in a place so isolated, they had to bring stuff in by air and only got mail once a week. As it was, she was at maximum capacity on the freak-out scale, so Hunter's latest revelation barely made a blip on her radar.

For the next half hour, neither of them spoke as Hunter radioed someone at the cattle station and she silently prayed not to die in a fiery crash. She tried to make out the ground, but everything around her was pitch black.

Darkness didn't really exist in New York City. Even at night, it tended to be fairly light. Right now, it felt like she'd been sucked into a giant black hole.

The egg-shaped helicopter reminded her of the old Humpty Dumpty nursery rhyme and the "had a great fall" line played over and over in her mind. She couldn't let go of the idea she was definitely spiraling out of control.

As the helicopter landed in the middle of a field, Annie took her first peaceful breath since waking, grateful to still be alive. She looked around but couldn't see much of the ranch in the darkness.

The same thought she'd had at the airport returned.

How the hell did I get here?

She wasn't sure what had possessed her to convince Hunter—a virtual stranger—to agree to take her over four hundred miles away from the airport and easy access to a return flight home. Clearly she had snapped.

"You can let go of that door handle." Hunter grinned. More dimples. He'd been very sweet earlier, distracting her with talk about family while trying to take her mind off the fact she was hovering far too high above the ground with nothing but propellers keeping her there. Her white-knuckle grip on the door hadn't relaxed since she'd woken up and heard they were about to land.

"I don't think I can." She wasn't joking, but Hunter chuckled just the same. He leaned over her, a whiff of his far-too-sexy cologne wafting in the air.

"Here." He gently pried each of her fingers away from the handle. Once her hand was free, he rubbed her palm, the massage easing the tingles there while creating some new ones in her girlie parts.

The breath she'd recovered upon landing was sucked away again. Hunter's face was close to hers and she recalled the kiss he'd given her at the airport. She wasn't sure she'd ever been the recipient of such a passionate, all-in sort of embrace. Hunter hadn't held back anything.

She moved an inch closer and licked her lips.

Hunter's gaze flew to her mouth. Did he know what she wanted? He moved the slightest bit nearer and she could smell peppermint on his breath. He'd offered her one at the beginning of the flight, claiming it calmed nervous stomachs. She could use a bit of that cure now. Their close proximity had her tummy doing major flip-flops. Maybe she could steal some of the flavor from *him*. She closed the distance between them even more.

Hunter still held her hand and his grip tightened slightly. Her eyes drifted shut, waiting, wishing, praying for his kiss.

Instead, Hunter sighed. "Fuck."

Her gaze lifted to his, confused.

"You're Dylan's girl, Annie. You're here for *him*."

She winced with the realization. She'd flown halfway around the world because of Dylan's friendship, his kindness, his sweet flirting. Didn't she owe it to him not to throw herself at his brother?

"I'm sorry. I've been traveling for two days and I'm not thinking straight. Nothing's gone the way I expected. I just..."

Hunter lifted her hand and placed a soft kiss on her palm. "No worries, love. We'll get a cup of hot tea and some supper in you. That cures everything."

"Food sounds nice."

Hunter unfastened her seatbelt. "I called ahead while you were sleeping. Told Mum you were with me. She's out of her head with excitement about meeting you."

"She is?" His words eased her initial anxiety about inconveniencing Mrs. Sullivan.

"She tried to convince Dylan to invite you here to

begin with, but Dylan said there was no way he could subject you to that long trip."

Annie laughed. "Bless Dylan for trying."

Hunter hopped out of the helicopter then came over to lift her out. She figured it was her pent-up sexual need that made her believe his hands lingered on her waist a second longer than necessary. Suddenly she was glad she'd thought to pack her vibrator. Something told her she was going to need it.

Hunter grabbed her luggage and led her from the landing pad to a jeep parked nearby. "The house is about a kilometer away."

"Damn metric system. I suppose that means it's close?"

Hunter chuckled. "Very close. Come on."

They rode the rest of the way to the Sullivan ranch house in silence. It was a dry, hot night and an odd smell—eucalyptus maybe?—hung in the air. She felt sticky beneath her long-sleeve sweater and jeans. She was dressed for late autumn in New York, not summer in Oz.

The jeep didn't have a top and the wind whipped through Annie's hair. She didn't even want to know what she looked like right now. So much for making a good impression on Hunter's mom.

When Hunter parked the jeep in front of the house, Annie tried to hastily finger-comb the mass of brown waves into submission, with little success. Hunter came around to her side of the vehicle.

"You look fine," he said.

"Dylan didn't tell me about your propensity for lying."

Hunter reached up and pushed a stray lock away from her face, tucking it behind her ear. Then he picked up where she'd left off on the grooming, running his fingers through her shoulder-length tresses. She didn't resist since he had the added benefit of actually seeing what he was doing.

"Mum will no doubt talk your ear off all through dinner. Maybe we should work out a signal. You can stomp on my foot or wink or something when you get too tired. I'll step in and insist you need a shower. I'll strong-arm you away from her and show you to the guest room, where you can take a long, hot bath and relax in silence. Sound like a plan?"

Annie nodded.

"Good girl. Come on."

AS THEY WALKED up the steps toward the front door, Annie nervously wiped her palms on her jeans.

Hunter reached over and took her hand. "There's nothing to be worried about."

He suspected that was true. While Hunter had talked his mouth dry trying to convince Dylan he was making a mistake flying to New York, their mother had proclaimed just the opposite. It was Mum who'd talked Dylan into signing up for the online dating service to begin with. In fact, she'd tried to convince both of them to try it, but Hunter had shot down the idea immediately.

Hunter's mother despaired of her sons ever finding a "good woman" to settle down with. Hazel Sullivan had regretfully come to the conclusion several years earlier that there were no neighboring women who were the right age or had the correct disposition for her boys.

Undeterred, she'd broadened her search. She had even gone so far once as to fly in potential candidates under the guise of hiring someone to work in the kitchen. Hunter had withstood the sexual advances of no less than six so-called station cooks before he cottoned on to his mother's game. The women had been nieces or daughters of dear friends; one was his mum's hairdresser's niece's best friend. Only one of them could actually fix anything mildly edible.

Finally, Hunter put his foot down and hired a cook himself. Bruce Hernan had been feeding the hands successfully for nearly a year now.

Hunter opened the front door and there stood Mum with Dylan's dog, Mutt.

Hazel behaved just as Hunter knew she would—the moment Annie crossed the threshold, his mother embraced her like she was some long-lost beloved daughter. Then she proceeded to tell her every embarrassing secret about Hunter and Dylan's childhood she could remember. Hazel took her on a tour of the living room, pointing out all the framed pictures of him and Dylan during various stages of growing up.

His mother was in fine form tonight. Poor Annie.

"And I've heard all about *you*," Annie said, bending down and petting Mutt. The dog was part dingo, part mythological beast. Hunter had protested the dog—even as a puppy—was too big to be a house pet, but when it became apparent the huge creature wouldn't part from Dylan's side, even at bedtime, the battle had been lost. Now it looked like Mutt had found a surrogate to guard during Dylan's absence, as the dog planted himself at Annie's feet.

Hazel watched Annie and the dog appraisingly. Annie had been nothing but courteous thus far, but Hunter could see his mother taking stock of the American. Hazel was one of the strongest women he'd ever known but her personality could be overwhelming for strangers. She was far too opinionated, spoke her mind and never minced words. While Annie was clearly tough in her own right,

Hunter had spent more than a few minutes of today's long, quiet flight wondering what Hazel would think of her.

He told himself his concern was on Dylan's behalf. If his brother was serious about Annie, he'd obviously want their mother's approval. That was a lie though. Hunter wanted the New Yorker and his mum to get along because he genuinely liked Annie.

After forty-five minutes of conversation and two cups of tea, he decided to throw her a lifeboat.

"Mum, I'm sure Annie's knackered and hungry. She's been traveling for nearly two days straight."

"Oh my goodness. Where are my manners?" Hazel rose quickly. "Dinner is in the oven and probably just about finished. Let me go check. I'll call you both in when it's on the table."

Hazel left Hunter alone with Annie. He walked over to sit beside her on the couch. "Sorry. Mum can be too much to handle at times."

"I think she's wonderful. She sure does love her sons."

Hunter grinned. "She loves us a bit *too* much."

Annie tried to stifle a yawn. The dark circles under her eyes told him exactly how exhausted she was.

"You more hungry or tired? You don't have to eat now if you'd rather get some sleep. I'm sure Mum won't mind if you come down later for a midnight bite to eat."

"Oh no," Annie said. "She's taken special pains to make the meal for me. I'm okay. I'd rather hang in there as long as possible. Figure it's the best way to get myself acclimated to this time zone."

He could see the reason in that, especially if she was serious about following around tomorrow as he did his chores. "I should warn you. The days start bloody early here on Farpoint. You still gung-ho on shadowing a stockman?"

She turned to face him, her knee brushing against his upper thigh. The light contact spurred a strong reaction. He'd been far too busy with work and too celibate lately. He needed to get laid…and soon, or he was bound to do something he'd regret. Like Annie.

"You're not going to get rid of me that easy. This is the first big assignment Mr. Lennon has given me. I'm not about to give up."

"I'd say that's pretty obvious, given the fact you got in a helicopter with a man you've never met and let him fly you to his home in the middle of nowhere."

Annie laughed and Hunter relished the sound. He tried to tell himself it was only attractive because there weren't a lot of available women his age at Farpoint, but he knew better. She had a nice laugh. And a pretty smile. And a gorgeous face.

Fuck.

"You have a very good point," she said. "I have no doubt my father will kill me when he hears where I am."

"Your dad doesn't know you're here?"

Annie shook her head. "As you pointed out, it was a pretty impulsive trip. I left a message with his secretary that I was traveling on assignment the morning I flew out, knowing he was in meetings all day."

"Coward," Hunter teased.

"When it comes to my dad, I've learned it's easier to apologize after than ask permission before."

"You need to ask permission? At your age?"

"It's just an expression. My dad's got a fairly strong personality so I've learned to avoid annoying confrontations by employing stealthy measures."

Was it Hunter's imagination or had Annie touched his thigh as she spoke? "Ah, so you're a bad girl."

During their conversation, they'd somehow managed

to move closer, the tenor of their words becoming more flirtatious.

Annie leaned even nearer. "I'm *very* good at being naughty."

"How naughty?"

She flushed, but didn't move away from him. They were treading a thin line between playful banter and outright seduction.

"I liked the way you kissed me in Sydney." It was a charming admission—and all Hunter needed to hear. He leaned forward and captured her lips. The kiss at the airport had merely whetted his desire for more.

Annie met him halfway, her mouth opening eagerly when he touched her lower lip with his tongue. For several minutes, they lived in the moment, all thought washed away by sensation and lust.

He pulled her shirt hem out of her pants and dipped his hand beneath, savoring the feeling of the warm skin at her waist. With one smooth motion, he pulled her over him until she straddled his thighs. Gripping her arse, he ground his cock against the vee of her legs. She moaned then added more pressure, gyrating against him sinuously until the friction was almost unbearable. During it all, their lips never parted.

Annie retreated first. "What are you doing to me?" Her whispered question was murmured against his mouth, her breathless gasps driving him back for another taste.

She didn't resist the second round, either; the longer, deeper kisses as they continued to rub against each other hard…harder.

Hunter was lightheaded with need. He gripped her face in his palms, holding her close. Her skin was soft, her breath sweet. When they parted again, he responded between panting breaths, "I think *I'm* the one who should be asking that question."

Annie froze and he watched her hooded, hungry eyes widen with shock as she realized what she was doing.

With regret, he let her crawl slowly off his lap, reclaiming her seat beside him. "I'm not usually quite this…forward."

He believed her. He felt the same. He'd only met her this morning and twice he'd held on to her like the world would end if she weren't snug in his arms. It was odd, unsettling.

"You're tired. You planned a trip and nothing's turned out the way you'd intended. I've had an unusual day too, a break from my same old, boring routine. I have a feeling things will be normal again after we've both had a good night's sleep." Christ. He hoped that was true. He'd been seconds from peeling Annie out of her jeans and fucking her senseless on the family couch with his mum in the next room.

Annie tilted her head. Hunter suspected she wanted to dispute his explanation. Instead, she said, "Maybe you're right."

Hazel called them in for dinner and the conversation turned into the interrogation Hunter had been waiting for. Hazel launched no less than three dozen questions at Annie. Their American guest answered all of his mother's questions regarding her schooling, her career at the magazine and her family with ease and even humor. Hunter noticed she didn't go into as much detail with Hazel, shielding some of the more private things she'd shared with him in the helicopter.

Hunter was pleased she'd told him more. He waited for Annie to give him one of the signs to call a halt to the third degree, but she never winked, never stomped on his foot.

Despite the dark circles and obvious tiredness in her eyes, Annie didn't try to break away from his mother's lengthy conversation.

"Mum, it's getting late. I'm going to take Annie and her luggage to the guest room so she can get a bath and some rest."

He expected Annie to look grateful for his reprieve, but instead she seemed disappointed to leave. Hazel shared the look.

"Forgive me, Annie, I've been terribly rude keeping you up so long."

"Not at all. I've enjoyed getting to know you. You have a lovely home, Mrs. Sullivan. I can't thank you enough for letting me stay. Is there anything worse than an unexpected guest showing up for a two-week visit?"

Mum waved Annie's words away with the flick of a wrist. "Nonsense. We're glad to have you. And none of this *Mrs. Sullivan* bull. Hazel will do just fine."

Annie and his mum hugged good night and Hunter led her to the guest room at the far end of the hall. Unfortunately it was right next to his bedroom, and his dick thickened at the thought of Annie sleeping only one thin wall away.

As they walked into the bedroom, he placed her luggage near the dresser. He pointed to a door in the corner. "The bathroom's in there. Knowing Mum, there are fresh towels and extra toiletries and God knows what else set up for you. I radioed the station about an hour after you fell asleep. Got an earful from Mum about not giving her enough notice."

"And yet she managed to make up this room and prepare a yummy dinner."

Hunter shrugged. "She wanted to make sure the place was nice for you."

"Your mother is…" Annie paused. Hunter held his breath, waiting for her to finish the thought. "She's just amazing. My mother left us when I was seven. Took off to Europe with a much younger lover. I only see her every three or four years at most."

"That must've been tough."

Annie shook her head. "Hard to miss what you never had." She looked toward the doorway. "But I think your mother made me miss what could have been."

Hunter couldn't stop himself from responding to Annie's wistful face. He walked over and hugged her. She accepted the embrace, wrapping her arms around his waist. "I'm glad you and Dylan fucked up the details."

Annie laughed. "I'm glad we did too."

He pulled away and resisted the urge to kiss her again. He'd already taken too many liberties, come on far too strong. While he was no stranger to one-night hookups, Annie wasn't that kind of woman. For one, she'd come here to meet Dylan, and secondly, she was staying in his family's home for two weeks.

Hunter knew all the way to his gut that it wasn't going to be long enough.

He needed to get in touch with Dylan.

Chapter Three

Annie carried a Vegemite sandwich wrapped in a paper towel to the shed for Hunter. She'd panicked a bit when she'd come to the kitchen for breakfast this morning and discovered he wasn't there. She was typically a fairly self-reliant person, but she felt like a fish out of water in Australia. Having Hunter around made things easier, less intimidating.

Hazel had put her at ease almost instantly at the breakfast table, entertaining her with funny stories about life at Farpoint. At least, Annie *thought* they were meant to be humorous. Mrs. Sullivan's Australian accent was rather thick and she tended to use some colorful expressions. Annie was still trying to piece out exactly what "dry as a dead dingo's donger" meant. She certainly had her suspicions, but still. It had been a bit shocking to hear, coming from the older woman's lips. She'd have to use that line with Monet one night. Her girlfriend would love it.

She glanced at the sandwich and wondered how anyone could voluntarily eat anything so vile. Dylan had mailed her some Vegemite a month ago. She'd taken one bite and spit the shit out, passing the jar on to Monet, who for some strange reason loved the stuff. Not wanting to be rude to Hunter's mother during her first breakfast in Oz, she'd forced herself to take a bite of the stuff on toast and swallow. Hazel had taken great pleasure in her discomfiture then complimented her for "hanging in there", swearing the flavor would grow on her, but Annie had no intentions of making a third attempt.

She entered a shed made almost entirely of corrugated iron. It was a far cry from the fancy wooden barns she'd seen during her travels in America. She'd mistakenly referred to it as a stable last night over dinner and Hunter had set her right once more. Stable, shed. Ranch, station. Cowboy, stockman. Potato, potahto. She'd never keep it all straight. Despite her exhaustion over dinner, it had been a comfortable, fun meal. Hazel and Hunter were hospitable and gracious.

Annie followed the sound of male voices toward the back wall. Hazel told her a cow was giving birth and Hunter had come down to help. She'd learned over breakfast that Hunter was less of a stockman than he'd led her to believe. According to Hazel, Dylan did more of the hands-on work around the property, while Hunter handled the business end. Where Dylan had a talent for buying stock—according to Hazel, he had a brilliant eye for picking prize cattle—Hunter spent most of his time in negotiations with banks and other buyers. Annie idly wondered why Hunter would keep that information from her.

She peered around the corner of a stall and found Hunter and another man kneeling by the laboring cow, who appeared to be in serious distress. The poor creature was breathing hard and every now and then she gave a low bellow. There was a slight odor in the air. Annie tried to place it.

Blood? *Ick.*

"Is she okay?"

Hunter glanced over his shoulder. He was wearing long plastic gloves that were covered in something shiny and gooey-looking. "The calf's a breech."

Annie knew the term, but wasn't sure what it meant in regards to cattle. "Can you do anything to help her?"

Hunter nodded. "Yeah. I'm trying. Do me a favor, Annie, go sit by her head and try to comfort her. We need to get the calf turned so he comes out. She's been laboring too long."

Annie placed the sandwich on a nearby stool then slowly dropped to her knees by the cow's head. She wasn't entirely sure what to do. She'd grown up with a couple of cats, and once, for her tenth birthday, her father had given her a toy poodle that she'd loved dearly. Reaching out, she stroked the cow's neck. It was a huge animal in comparison to Annie's small house pets or even Dylan's Mutt, but the cow acknowledged her touch, her chocolate-brown gaze taking in Annie's face.

She began to murmur soothing sounds as Hunter and the other hand conferred on what to do.

"Hush," she said softly. "It'll be okay." At least she thought so—until she watched Hunter put his hand inside the cow.

"Holy fuck."

Hunter glanced up at her exclamation, grimacing as he continued to reach around inside the cow. He was elbow-deep. Annie felt lightheaded.

"Sorry," he said through clenched teeth. "This calf's not going to come out without some help. This would be easier to do if the mother would stand, but she's worn out. That's why we need to move quickly."

"What are you doing?" she asked.

Hunter continued to work and Annie swallowed against the bile gathering in her throat. The sight of blood had always made her queasy, but this…

A bead of sweat rolled down the side of Hunter's face. "I'm trying to get the calf's front legs facing forward. If I can do that, she may be able to push the babe out herself."

"She's having another contraction," the other man said. "You think we need to consider pulling him?"

"Not yet," Hunter said. "That's the last resort. I'd like to give her a chance to deliver him without the strap."

"Strap?" Annie whispered.

"It's not as dire as it sounds," the other man assured her. "If Hunter can't get the calf in the right position, we put a nylon strap around both of the calf's legs and pull a little. Help things along."

Hunter continued whatever he was doing inside the cow. Annie patted the mother again, murmuring more words of comfort. She suspected her comments weren't just keeping the mother calm. Hunter seemed to take solace in them as well. He gave her a grateful smile as he tried to move the calf.

"I'm glad you're here, Annie."

Annie imagined her sisters' faces if they could see her now. She was in a barn in Australia, petting a cow, while Hunter had his hand somewhere Annie would never dream of sticking her own. What a day.

"Okay. It's coming." Hunter removed his arm and Annie leaned closer, trying to get a better look. She'd never seen anything born in her life—not an animal or a baby—and she was absolutely fascinated, despite the blood.

Soon, legs appeared, then a nose, a head. The cow

continued to strain until finally, amazingly, the calf emerged.

"Get me straw, Annie," Hunter said as he reached for a towel. Annie grabbed a handful of hay.

Hunter took a single piece. "Just one will work." He tickled the calf's nostrils as it started to breathe on its own.

Annie gasped when the tiny creature began to move. He was okay. The calf was alive. She'd never seen anything so incredible in her life. "It's a cow!"

Hunter glanced at her and grinned. "A male cow."

"A boy," Annie said with wonder. "We'll have to go out and buy blue."

The other hand gave her a funny look. "Where are you from, love?"

Hunter chuckled at the man's question. "Marc Thompson, this is Annie Prince, from America. New York."

"New York?" Marc asked. "Isn't that where Dylan went?"

Annie nodded but didn't add more. She wasn't sure how much the hands on Farpoint knew about her and Dylan, didn't know how much Hunter wanted to share with them.

Marc chuckled, his blue eyes shining with a light Annie recognized as mischief. "There's no bloody way I'd take off halfway 'round the world for a woman. Even if she *was* as pretty as Dylan reckoned."

Annie's belly knotted a little at the hand's words.

Hunter let out a low sound, and to Annie's ears it sounded like a growl. "That's enough, Thomo."

Marc grinned, dropping Annie a cheeky wink. "Although I gotta admit, the accent's bloody sexy. Say something else for me, Annie Prince."

Annie blinked, unsure how to react. Australian men unsettled her at times, their sense of humor hard to get a handle on. She suspected Marc was teasing her in a friendly way—at least the easy way he smiled at her indicated such—but she wasn't sure. The hands on Farpoint really didn't know who she was. Maybe he was flirting with her?

She cleared her throat, flicked Hunter a quick look and then gave the waiting cowboy a smile. "Wanna get some cawfee from Starrbucks, Marc?" she asked, turning on her most New York accent.

Marc threw back his head and laughed, a relaxed sound that echoed around the shed. Annie noticed the hint of ink peeking from under the open collar of his shirt, but what the tat was, she couldn't tell.

"Oh, that does it for me, baby." He grinned at her. "Any chance you wanna crawl into my bed tonight and talk in that sexy accent some more?"

"Settle down, Thompson," Hunter said. "You'll give us Aussie blokes a bad name."

Marc flashed another grin at Annie. "Me? Nah. Besides, I'm not the typical Aussie bloke."

Hunter snorted. "That's for certain." He shook his head. "Do you carry on like this when Dylan's around?"

Marc burst out laughing again. "Hell no."

Hunter groaned. "Then shut the hell up now and pretend I'm the boss out here for a while, will you? I'm the one who had my hands elbow-deep in cow, you know."

Marc tapped the brim of his hat with a finger, dropping Annie another wink. "Can do, boss."

Annie found herself smiling. She couldn't help it. The whole tête-à-tête was so bizarrely unexpected and fun.

Marc pointed to the calf. "You ever seen a calf born?"

Annie shook her head. "Not a lot of cows in Manhattan."

"Well, we appreciate your help, even if you are a

Yank," Marc teased. "In fact, I think maybe we should mark the occasion somehow, since it's your first time." Marc looked at Hunter. "How about we call this little fella Prince in honor of our assistant?"

"I didn't do anything," Annie insisted.

Hunter winked at her. "You did plenty. And I think that's a great idea, Marc." Hunter bent over and placed his hand on the newborn calf's nose. "I hereby dub you, Prince."

Annie felt her throat tighten, touched by the sweet gesture.

Hunter walked over to her. "I'd help you up, but…"

He lifted his slimy, glove-covered hands and she crinkled her nose. "No thanks." She stood and followed him to a large sink behind the stable. They took turns washing their hands.

"So what did you think of that?" Hunter asked.

"It was the most fascinating, scary, exciting thing I've ever seen. I can't wait to write about it."

Hunter handed her a towel. "You're right. It *is* all those things. I'd forgotten."

"How could you forget that?"

Hunter shrugged. "Seeing a calf born isn't a new thing for me. Happens pretty often around here. I guess I've let the wonder of the moment slip away. You just gave it back to me."

Annie smiled, pleased. Hunter was clearly born to the right place, the right time. It was a concept she'd considered a lot lately. She'd never felt like she fit in her family, her home. Annie wished there was someplace where she could feel a sense of belonging. She envied Hunter that. He belonged on Farpoint Creek.

"Hey, boss," Marc called from the shed. "I think we've got a problem."

Annie's heart dropped. "Prince."

They rushed back into the stable. The mother had risen and was standing in a corner, away from her new baby.

"She's rejecting it," Hunter said.

"What's that mean?"

Hunter shrugged. "Just what it sounds like."

Marc was in the process of cleaning the calf. "Ordinarily the mother will do this, but she's not feeling too kindly toward the little thing right now."

Hunter sighed. "Dylan would push this issue, right?"

Marc nodded. "I can tie her up, pen her in with Prince, but she's pretty anxious right now. I'd hate to see her hurt the calf."

Hunter was quiet for a few minutes as he watched the mother. "Get a bottle, Marc. We can feed Prince that way until the mother calms down a bit."

Marc's face cleared and Annie knew he approved of Hunter's decision.

"Is this normal?" she asked.

Hunter grasped her hand, tugging her close enough that he could wrap his arm around her shoulders. She'd never been with a man who held her hand, hugged and kissed her so often. It was as if he couldn't keep his hands off her. Annie liked it. A lot.

"It's not unheard of in difficult births. Or even easy ones, for that matter. There are ways to get the mother to accept the baby, but I think we'll give them both a rest for right now."

Marc came back with a large bottle. Hunter handed it to Annie. "You want to feed Prince while Marc and I get some clean straw for that stall? Our little calf and his mother are going to stay in here for a few days."

Annie took the bottle and looked at the newborn calf.

"Um. Okay. Sure." She sat next to the baby and coaxed him to suck on the bottle.

Hunter ruffled Annie's hair. "You're a born jillaroo."

She snorted. "Did you just make that word up?"

Hunter shook his head. "Nope. It's a real one. Means you were born to work on a station. What you Americans call a ranch hand. But a girl one. A jackaroo is a bloke. A jillaroo is…well, you get the drift."

Hunter and Marc left her alone in the stable with Prince. As the calf suckled, Annie sighed contentedly. She could see the appeal of this lifestyle. It was peaceful at Farpoint. No horns blaring, people yelling, construction work. No paparazzi following her, cameras flashing, phones ringing. Nothing but quiet, blissful silence.

She stroked the calf's head. "You'll be okay," she murmured softly. "Your mommy's just tired. She's still here. She won't leave you forever." Annie swallowed hard against the lump forming in her throat. "And if she does, you'll be okay because I'll take care of you. I know what it's like to lose a mother. I won't let you feel lonely, okay, Prince?"

HUNTER STOOD at the back door of the equipment shed and listened to Annie's promise. She'd mentioned her mother's desertion, acted like the event was nothing, no big deal. He saw through that act now. Annie felt her mother's rejection deeply. Hunter longed to go to her, but he didn't think she'd thank him for eavesdropping.

A slight movement by one of the front stalls caught his attention. His mum's gaze captured his and he could tell by the upset look on her face, she'd heard Annie too.

She jerked her head to the right, indicating she wanted to talk to him. Hunter nodded silently then walked around the outside of the shed, not wanting to disturb Annie. His mother met him at the front doors, beside the main water tank.

"Dylan called."

Hunter glanced toward the house. "Is he still on the phone?"

"No. He rang while you were delivering the calf. I told him Annie was here and safe. Told him not to worry because you were taking good care of her."

Hunter thought his mother's tone was almost hopeful, but he dismissed it as wishful thinking on his part. Hazel wouldn't condone him trying to steal his brother's gal.

"Shit. I was hoping to speak to him."

Hazel nodded. "I told him you'd ring later."

"Is he headed back?"

Hazel shook her head. "No. Airline lost his luggage. He's staying there until they find it."

Hunter rubbed his eyes wearily. Resisting Annie would be a lot easier when Dylan was back. At least…he hoped it would be.

Annie walked out of the shed, covering her mouth with a yawn neither he nor his mother missed.

"You working Annie too hard today, Hunter? Poor girl hasn't even recovered from her trip and you've got her pulling calves in labor and delivery."

Annie gave him a teasing grin. "He's a taskmaster, Hazel. A regular slave driver."

Hunter crossed his arms and feigned annoyance. "Great. Typical of Dylan to head across the pond and bloody well leave me here outnumbered and surrounded by sheilas who think they're funny."

Hazel laughed. "Drop it, boyo. Sheila? When was the last time anyone in this century used the term 'sheila'? I think you're bunging on an act for our guest here." She wrapped her arm around Annie's shoulders. "The best thing for you is a quick lunch and then a nap. It's going to take you a few days to get your internal clock sorted. After you wake up, you can help me in the kitchen. I'm baking a cake for the Country Women's Association. We're meeting tonight for a potluck dinner."

"Country Women?" Annie asked.

Hazel nodded. "It's a meeting of all the wives who live at Farpoint."

"It's an excuse to eat too much, drink a lot of wine and gossip," Hunter clarified.

Annie's face brightened. "Ooo...wine. That sounds great."

"You're welcome to come with me. You could include it in that article you're writing about us." Hazel had been far too pleased and willing to help when she'd learned about Annie's series on Farpoint. If there was one thing his mum was proud of, it was her home. The idea of an American magazine featuring a story about them thrilled her to no end.

"I'd love to go. If you're certain I won't be imposing."

"Not at all, my dear. We'd love to have you. In fact, our schoolteacher, Amy, will be over the moon to meet you. Though I fear she'll pepper you with a thousand and two questions about New York. That girl is America-mad." Hazel turned her toward the house and the two of them began to walk away.

Annie glanced back at Hunter. He tried to ignore the longing in her eyes, but he couldn't deny it was there. Couldn't pretend the same look was probably lingering in his gaze. She'd brightened up his morning—and the previous evening, making him feel things he hadn't felt in a very long time. The foolish sentiment made him feel like a green-around-the-gills teenager again.

They were treading a dangerous path.

He waved. "Go on and sleep. I'm going to finish up a few things in the shed, then tackle some paperwork in my office. I'll see you before you head out to the meeting."

"Okay."

Hunter watched Annie and his mum walk to the house, the two women talking away like long-lost sisters. Hazel had embraced the New Yorker, taking her under her wing, and he was struck by how lonely his mum must be at the homestead with only him and Dylan for company.

True, there were other women on Farpoint. Hell, the station was now big enough to have its own school for the hired hands' little kids. The teacher, Amy Wesson, spent quite a bit of time with Hazel. But Amy was young and the hired hands' wives treated Hazel like the boss she actually was, as did the jillaroos. Until Annie appeared, he'd never seen his mum so…happy. And chatty.

Hunter let out a ragged breath.

Annie was good for Hazel.

She was good for all of them.

Chapter Four

Annie splashed her face with water from the trough, relishing the bite of the chill. She was sweating her ass off. It was the end of November, typically the beginning of winter in New York, and she was standing in the middle of a desert with sweat rolling down her back. Her muscles were sore from helping Hunter with some of the chores he said were common tasks on the station. She'd met quite a few of the jackaroos—and even a few jillaroos—who worked for the Sullivans. Farpoint Creek was clearly a large and important cattle station, given the sheer number of men and women who lived and worked on the land.

She'd recorded hours of interviews and conversations and tried to list key points she didn't want to forget to include in her writing. Several times she'd been so caught up in the moment, she'd completely forgotten to record or note *anything*, so she'd have to rely on her memory for some things when it came time to prepare her articles. There was simply too much going on all the time.

"Feel better?" Hunter asked.

She nodded. It was only her third day on the station.

Three very busy, crazy, work-filled days. "It's so hot."

Hunter grinned. "Oh love, this isn't hot. Summer hasn't even started to kick in yet."

"Holy shit. How can you stand it?"

Hunter shrugged as he handed her a towel to dry her face. She'd given up trying to wear makeup during the day. It was pointless considering she'd simply sweat it all off before noon. Given the way Hunter was looking at her, he didn't appear to mind her au naturale appearance.

Hunter picked up the wide-brimmed Akubra Hazel had loaned her and put it back on her head. "We find ways to beat the heat. Speaking of, you've been working hard the last couple of days. Why don't I show you more of the station? So far most of your chores have been around the homestead. I'll give you a tour and," he lifted a large bag she hadn't noticed before, "even throw a picnic in as part of the deal."

Annie's stomach rumbled hungrily. "Food sounds awesome." She'd found her appetite in Australia. Never a big eater at home, she typically existed on salads and yogurt. Since her arrival at Farpoint, she'd worked up a hunger she didn't know existed. Hazel had invited her to help make dinner last night, sharing recipes and cooking tips. Growing up with a household cook who considered the kitchen his sacred property, Annie had never been exposed to the joys of cooking and baking.

Last night, she and Hazel had turned up an oldies station on the radio and danced around in aprons while baking fresh rolls for dinner and a pecan pie for dessert. She smiled at the memory.

"So let's talk about your skills on a horse."

Her smile disappeared. "You mean like *riding* one?"

Hunter nodded.

"We're not going to take the ute?" Annie smiled again,

proud of her use of the unique Australian word. Why they didn't just say "pickup" was beyond her, but she liked the way *ute* sounded in her mouth. She was discovering she liked a lot of things about Australia.

He grasped her hand and tugged her toward the stable. "I'll take that to mean you're not a horsewoman."

"That would be a very good assumption to make."

They reached the shed just as Frankie, a young hand she'd met the previous day, came out with a saddled horse. Hunter took the reins from him.

"Thanks, mate."

Annie peered behind Frankie. "Only one horse? Were you that sure of my answer?"

Hunter winked at her. "You mentioned a lack of cows in Manhattan. I assumed the same held true for other four-legged creatures."

Annie put her hands on her hips. "I'll have you know there are tons of horses in the city."

"Really?"

She nodded. "There are horse-drawn buggies in Central Park and policemen who patrol the streets on horses."

"I stand corrected then. Does this mean you want to ride alone rather than behind me?"

She glanced at the large animal and considered trying to control something so powerful on her own. Her gaze drifted back to Hunter's muscular form and she licked her lips. He was certainly a strong creature she'd like to ride, though she suspected she wouldn't have much more luck controlling *him*. Not that she'd mind that much. Visions of Hunter lying beneath her on the bed as she straddled his hips flashed before her eyes, and suddenly it wasn't just sweat that was leaving her wet and sticky.

"Earth to Annie."

She blinked rapidly, her vision focusing on Hunter as he waved his hand in front of her face.

"You still with me?"

She flushed, heat rising to her already too-warm face. "Sorry. Um. Zoned out. I think I'd rather ride with you." The admission on the heels of her sex fantasy sent her mind straight back to the gutter, and she imagined Hunter's fingers gripping her ass, urging her to go faster, harder.

Hunter gave her a funny look and she prayed he couldn't read minds. He put their lunch in a pack attached to the back of the saddle, then mounted the horse.

Reaching down, he offered her a hand. "Put your left foot in the stirrup. I'll pull you up."

She placed her hand in his, marveling at the strength in his grasp. She'd never known such a physically powerful man. The men she'd dated in the city tended to be slimmer, more lean than muscular. Their hands hadn't been rough with calluses, like Hunter's.

His skin wore a natural golden tan she suspected was there year-round. She bet he never succumbed to the winter-white complexion that plagued most New Yorkers during the long, snowy months.

Once she was seated behind him, she knew she was in for a long afternoon of unending horniness. Her crotch was snug against his far-too-sexy ass and when he grasped her hands and pulled them around his waist, she clasped them together quickly, lest she be tempted to rest them somewhat lower.

"All right then?" he asked.

She nodded, tightening her grip as he flicked the reins and the horse began to move. They rode in silence for several minutes as Annie tried to batten down her physical urges. Hunter had made it clear nothing could happen between them. She'd come here to meet Dylan, though that reason seemed to matter less with each passing hour. In fact, she'd tried to call Monet the previous day, but the time difference and life weren't being very kind to her. She recalled the message she'd left on Monnie's machine and winced. Her friend would think she'd gone mental.

"Hi Monnie. I just…I just wanted to say hi. Australia is amazing. Hunter is…has been showing me the station. I hope Dylan is okay. I really need to talk to him. There's something I need to… I really need to talk to him. Please tell him I said hello. I hope you're looking after him. Love you."

While she and Dylan had formed a fun friendship, complete with flirting, she didn't think either of them had seriously engaged feelings. At least, *she* didn't. She wasn't sure about Dylan, but she needed to find out…and soon. Hunter's hesitance to give in to the mutual attraction between them made her wonder if Dylan had said something about their online relationship being more serious.

Annie had jumped at the chance to travel to Australia because—in addition to wanting to meet Dylan in person —she'd wanted to get the hell out of the city before the Thanksgiving holiday kicked in. She needed a break from her family, her job, the paparazzi.

She glanced around. There wasn't a single camera pointed at her, no one following her, shouting questions and inappropriate comments. For the moment, it was as if she and Hunter were the only two people on the planet.

Despite the ungodly heat and flies, she was starting to believe she'd found heaven on earth.

Hunter broke the silence first as he gestured to some outbuildings, explaining the purpose of each. As they rode, he pointed out various things—fencing, cattle grazing, trails they used for four-wheeling. The land was beautiful, isolated but useful. Everything seemed to have a purpose, a reason for being, and once again Annie felt like the stray piece of a puzzle, the one that didn't fit.

She pushed the thought away. There wasn't room for that today. She was too happy and unwilling to let go of that emotion.

They rode for nearly an hour as Hunter told her stories about growing up on the cattle station. She'd been shocked to learn he hadn't gone to a proper school. Instead, his education had been achieved by some School in the Air, a rather bizarre concept where all the kids communicated with their teacher via radio. As he spoke, she marveled over how different their lives were. And yet, for some odd reason, she felt more connected to this stockman than she did with her friends from home, or even her sisters.

"Oh look," she said, pointing to her right. "A lake."

Hunter glanced over his shoulder. "That's where we've been heading all this time. And love, that's a *billabong*."

He directed the horse toward a clearing. Hopping down, he reached up for her. Annie leaned forward, placing her trust in Hunter as he caught her, delivering her safely to the ground. He kept his arms around her as she struggled to find her footing.

"My legs are wiggly."

He laughed at her description. "You're not used to spending so much time on horseback. It gets easier."

Once she'd gotten her sea legs back, Hunter released her, grabbing their lunch and a large blanket from the pack.

Annie walked closer to the water, enjoying the fresh, clean air and smell of wet earth. It was a welcome change after several days spent in the dry heat surrounding the homestead.

"It's beautiful here."

Hunter spread out the blanket and sat down. He patted

the spot next to him. "Hope you're hungry. Mum packed enough food for an army. You like roast beef sandwiches?"

She nodded.

"After we eat, we can take a dip if you want."

"I didn't bring a bathing suit."

Hunter gave her a wicked grin. "Skivvies work just as well."

She narrowed her eyes. "You expected me to swim in my underwear?"

"Why not? What's a bikini if not a bra and undies? Of course, if you prefer, skinny-dipping works too. I just figured you might be a bit modest."

She picked up a grape and threw it at his head. He dodged the tiny missile. "We'll sort out the details after we eat. I'm starving."

They chatted easily as they consumed Hazel's delicious food, but Hunter had planted a dangerous seed. Too many times during the meal, Annie wondered if Hunter was serious about skinny-dipping. Would she do it if he asked? Could she? She didn't consider herself shy by any stretch of the imagination, but Hunter wasn't exactly a friend daring her as a lark.

She'd seen the way he looked at her, knew his feelings were no more platonic than hers.

"So what made you pick Dylan out of all the men in that online dating pool?"

Hunter's question caught her off-guard, but suddenly she felt grateful for the chance to explain her reasons for signing up. He'd said enough over the past two days to give her the feeling he wasn't a fan of finding true love virtually.

"Actually, I didn't. My friend, Monet, was the one who spotted him. We were having a girls night, drinking wine, commiserating over my latest in a long line of shitty boyfriends. Next thing I know, Monet's signing me up for the service, insisting that there was someone, somewhere in the world, who could love me for me and not my family's money."

Hunter scowled. "You been dating gold diggers?"

"Well, not by choice. Usually their true natures and reasons for going out with me don't come out until much later in the relationship. Might be better to say I date actors. Even if they have other jobs, I always manage to find men who are very convincing when it comes to their interest in me."

"New York men sound like wankers."

She glanced at the lake, grinning. "Not all of them. I've actually dated some really nice guys too. Unfortunately those are invariably the ones I feel zero attraction to."

"So if Monet picked Dylan, how did *you* end up talking to him?"

"She picked him out for *me*. We were three sheets to the wind and Monet gave him my email. One thing sort of led to another and before I knew it, we were emailing back and forth every day."

"What did you two talk about?"

Annie shrugged. "Nothing deep, really. Our jobs, families, what we ate for breakfast. Silly stuff. Dylan's a really easy guy to talk to. He was nice and," she paused, trying to find the right word, "safe."

"What's that mean?"

Annie wiped her mouth and pushed away the paper plate. Once again, she'd eaten enough to choke a horse. If she stayed in Australia much longer, she'd have to start jogging to keep off the extra weight. "Dylan was half a world away. It's easy to flirt with someone you run very little risk of ever seeing in person."

"But you agreed to meet him."

She nodded. Dylan's invitation had come on a very bad

day. Her boss had called her "Princess" during a staff meeting, Joel had found a new rich girlfriend, telling the tabloids Annie's cold-fish tendencies in the bedroom led to their breakup, and her sister, Cindy, had called to inform her that their Thanksgiving meal was going to be recorded for a special holiday event on the reality show. "When I read that IM from Dylan, I was feeling pretty lonely. Getting out of town seemed like the answer to a prayer."

Hunter began clearing up their food, placing the leftovers back in the bag. "So did you come here for Dylan… or a vacation with benefits?"

It was a good question. She wished she had a better answer. "Both, I guess. I thought I'd see if the fun that Dylan and I had online translated into real life, *and* I wanted to get away. Desperately."

Hunter studied her face for a long time and she wondered if her response pissed him off. It wasn't the first time she'd had to wonder if Dylan's feelings had been more strongly engaged. What if, by admitting her real reasons for coming, Hunter now saw her as a user? A woman looking for a fling while escaping her real life? She hadn't painted a very pretty picture of herself.

The silence unnerved her. She stood and walked back toward the lake. Taking off her hat, she fanned herself with it while finger-combing her hair. A rumble caught her attention and she glanced up to discover a dark cloud overhead.

"Damn. Storm coming."

She turned, surprised to see Hunter standing so close behind her. A quick look showed that he'd folded up the blanket and put it and the food back in the pack.

She was sorry to leave. "I guess we should head back."

He nodded, looking up. "Not sure we're going to beat it. Think we're about to get pissed on from a great height."

As if he'd dared the gods, rain began to fall. Unlike the storms at home, this one skipped the drizzle and got straight to the good part.

Sheets of water fell, soaking her in an instant. The quick, unexpected change caught her unaware and her mouth fell open.

Hunter wiped his eyes. Grinning, he shook his head and shrugged. "Looks like a belly washer."

Annie had never found pleasure in rain. In New York, the skies would go dark and gray for days on end, never producing more than a few measly icy-cold drops at a time. This rain felt different. It cooled her overheated skin, washing away the sweat, the grime, the smell of the horse. It was like bathing in a beautiful waterfall.

She lifted her arms and spun around. "It's incredible!"

Hunter watched her with humor in his eyes. "It's just rain, you bloody crazy Yank."

"Maybe. But it feels so good."

Hunter's laughter died as his eyes drifted over her body hungrily. She glanced down and suddenly understood why men loved wet t-shirt contests so much. Her white shirt was sheer and it clung to her body, revealing every curve she possessed.

Her nipples were dark and erect. She wanted to blame it on the sudden chill, but she knew it had more to do with arousal.

Hunter had removed his hat and his hair was slick, wet. He pushed it away from his face.

She lowered her arms as both of them continued to stare at each other.

Then they moved at the same time.

Annie didn't have time to consider her actions when Hunter's arms wrapped around her waist, pulling her close. She gripped his face, forcing his lips to hers.

Hunter's kiss was hot and deep, passionate. Annie turned her head, trying to get more of him. They'd curbed one hunger with food. Now they were satisfying a different kind of starvation.

She ran her hands over his shoulders, dragging her fingers along his muscular arms. Hunter lifted his palms to her breasts, encapsulating her flesh with his large hands. He squeezed them and she moaned into his mouth.

The storm continued to pound down, but the force of the rain only drove their needs higher. Annie reached around Hunter and grasped his ass, her fingers digging into his jeans, pushing his erection against her stomach.

She longed to feel him inside her. Hunter pinched her nipples, the sharp, pleasurable pain sending shards of arousal to her pussy. She pulled away from the kiss slightly and gasped, but Hunter drew her back, refusing to free her lips.

Water dripped from their clothing. Annie gripped his soaked jeans tighter. She needed more than this. Tugging at the hem of his t-shirt, she untucked it and slipped her hands beneath. Bare, smooth skin met her fingertips. Hunter hissed when her chilled hands stroked his nipples, but he didn't break the union of their lips.

His tongue tangled with hers, then he nipped her lower lip. She returned the sensual attack. Hunter's fingers twisted in her hair. He tightened his hold, pulling the tresses until she thought she'd explode. So fucking good. So hot.

She'd spent a lifetime dreaming of a kiss like this, never finding a man who wanted her with a mindless, uncontrollable passion that could match hers. Annie dragged her nails along Hunter's chest, desperate to mark him, to scratch this moment permanently into his skin, his memory.

A flash of lightning pierced the darkness and Annie panicked. The bright light reminded her too much of a camera. It drove her back to the present, to reality, and she stepped away, glancing around. What if someone had seen? Taken a picture? Stolen the most precious moment of her life for their own financial gain?

"Fuck," Hunter muttered. His chest rose and fell, his breathing as labored as hers. "I'm so sorry, Annie."

Sorry? She was the one who'd had the ridiculous moment of panic. They truly were alone. As soon as she realized that, she regretted her foolishness. She missed his lips, his arms around her.

Before she could explain, Hunter bent down to pick up their hats, slapping them against his thighs. "I'd never do anything to hurt Dylan. It's just…"

Oh God. Dylan. She'd completely forgotten about Hunter's brother. "Hunter…" She needed to find a way around his feelings of guilt. She hadn't gotten a sense Dylan's feelings were any stronger than hers, but what if she'd misread their flirting, thinking it harmless, sexy, while Dylan put more stock into its meaning? What happened if he came home and expected more than she was able to give?

"We need to head to the homestead. The storm looks like it's dying, but that doesn't mean it won't come back worse. We shouldn't be out here in the lightning."

She nodded, feeling very weary and confused. Her clothes clung to her, suddenly cold and uncomfortable. She needed a hot bath and a long cry.

WHEN HUNTER and Annie arrived at the house, Hazel was on the front porch. The rain had slowed down considerably during their return trip. Hunter stopped near the house and hopped down, helping Annie descend.

She hadn't spoken a word since he'd kissed her by the billabong. Guilt lingered, but if given the chance, he'd drag Annie back into his arms again. He couldn't resist her, the pull growing stronger with each passing day.

Hazel started to speak, but stopped as her gaze traveled from Annie to him. Hunter's hands still lingered on Annie's waist in a far-too-familiar way. He fought to restrain his wince as he released her and took one step away. His mother was far too canny, too clever.

He rubbed his jaw, his fingers grazing his own lower lip. For the first time he tasted the slight tang of blood and he remembered Annie biting him. She was a wildcat, and he ached to unleash the sexy beast inside her.

Hazel took Annie's hand as she climbed the stairs. "You're soaked to the skin, dear girl. Why don't you go to your room and take a hot shower, get some dry clothes?"

Annie accepted Hazel's hand. "I might lie down too. Not sure when this jetlag will go away once and for all, but I'm sort of tired."

Hazel smiled kindly. "A nap should do the trick. Why don't you rest until dinner?"

Annie continued to the front door, turning before entering the house. "Thanks for the picnic, Hunter. Maybe we can do it again sometime."

He smiled. He'd thought her silence was based on regret. Now he wasn't so sure. "I'd like that."

"So would I."

Her words and her face, the direct way she looked him straight in the eye, told him she meant what she was saying.

She walked into the house.

He'd forgotten his mother was there until she spoke. "You need to call Dylan."

"I know. I will." Dylan had left a message on the answering machine the night before last, but Hunter hadn't returned the call, uncertain what to say. He'd considered ringing Dylan at least half a dozen times yesterday, but he and Annie had been having too much fun, so again, he avoided the issue. What would he do if Dylan said he was on his way home…coming back for Annie?

Hazel wasn't appeased. "When?"

"I need to take care of Jamboree first. The poor horse is soaking wet and—"

"Hunter. I'm not blind and I'm not stupid."

He knew that. "Mum, I'm going to call him. I promise."

Hazel nodded, then walked back into the house. Hunter led Jamboree back to the shed as he considered what he'd say to Dylan. How could he explain that the woman he'd accused his brother of acting like a fool over had shown up and tossed his world on its ear? Dylan wasn't just his brother, he was his mate, his best friend. Was he willing to risk that relationship over a woman he'd just met?

The ache in Hunter's chest made him very sad to recognize he might.

Fuck it. He'd never been afraid to talk to his brother before. It was time Hunter stopped acting like such a chicken shit. He quickly finished cleaning the horse then retrieved the leftover food from the pack.

As he strode to the house, he tried to clear his head, calm his nerves. Walking in the front door, he dropped the bag of food and picked up the phone. His mind was blank as he dialed the number. He listened to it ring, struggling to find one fucking word to say after "hello".

What *could* he say?

Hey Dylan, I know you're so crazy about Annie you traveled halfway around the bloody world to meet her, but would you mind giving up your potential soul mate so I can ask her out?

Hunter grimaced. Yeah. That would work. The phone continued to ring. He could always blow off the emotional attraction he felt toward her and make it about something less intimidating. He and Dylan were never shy about discussing the details of their sexual exploits.

Dylan, Annie's so fucking hot I can't keep my hands off her. She makes my dick throb so hard it's a wonder I haven't split the front of every pair of jeans I own. Would you mind if I drag her to bed and keep her there for a few weeks?

Bloody hell. Just the thought of saying that felt wrong. He wanted more from her than a mere fuck or two. That was the *real* problem.

All the arguments he'd laid out for Dylan on the way to Sydney International crashed down on his head. She's an American. She lives half a world away. No woman from New York City is going to want to settle down in the middle of the Outback. It's a waste of time, effort and emotion. A no-win situation.

Dylan—the king of living in the moment—hadn't had any answers to offer and hadn't seemed concerned about finding them. He'd wanted to meet Annie and he'd found a way to make it happen. Hunter wished he could do the same, but it wasn't in his nature. Where Dylan was a romantic bastard who leapt feet first, thinking of the consequences after the fact, Hunter was too fucking practical, a realist in every sense of the word.

Dylan's voice sounded through the phone and Hunter's heart seized before he realized it was voicemail. He considered what he wanted to say once more. Then he simply said, "Dylan. It's Hunter. Call me. We need to talk."

Chapter Five

Annie glanced at the clock. She was exhausted from tossing and turning, struggling to find sleep for nearly two hours. Her earlier nap had given her a cursed second wind. It also didn't help that Hunter had fired up her libido to dangerous levels on that picnic. She was a ticking time bomb of horniness.

The house had gone completely quiet nearly an hour ago. Hunter was in his office and she hadn't heard him return to his room yet. He must be burning the midnight oil.

Or maybe he was feeling as restless and needy as she was. She wondered if he'd take care of those needs on his own. She imagined him sitting at his desk, opening his pants and taking his cock in his hand. She grew wet as she imagined him stroking the thick flesh. He'd pressed his erection against her enough the past few days to convince her that he wasn't hurting in the penis department. Would he stroke it slowly, savoring each tight press? Or was he a hard-and-fast man, moving his hand with quick thrusts that caused his breathing to stutter and his eyes to close in sweet agony?

God. She forced the image away and pressed her legs together tightly. She'd never get to sleep at this rate. After rising from her nap, Annie had enjoyed another relaxing meal with mother and son, then spent the rest of the evening with Hunter in the office. She'd set up her laptop on the opposite side of his large desk and worked on her Farpoint article while he'd attended to the cattle station's ledgers. She'd enjoyed that quiet time with him almost as much as the tumultuous kisses in the rain.

Slowly it dawned on her it didn't matter where they were or what they were doing. When she was with Hunter, she felt…comfortable in her own skin, at peace. It was a new experience for her.

She lay still, listening once more to the silence. Finally she couldn't stand the ache in her pussy any longer. She tiptoed from the bed and rummaged through her luggage in the dark. Fortunately there was enough moonlight to help her find her vibrator. God willing, no one would hear the buzzing sound.

Returning to bed, she pulled off her t-shirt and panties. Lying down, she closed her eyes and softly stroked her clit, recalling the kiss Hunter had given her earlier.

He'd pushed her away out of respect for his brother and she admired him for his loyalty. Unfortunately, that kindness added one more tick to the *Ohmigod, this is why I want to fuck Hunter* list. In a few days, he'd racked up at least a dozen or more of those marks, which had all contributed to her current state. She rubbed herself harder and moaned softly.

Her pussy—already damp—turned molten as she imagined Hunter's face. He was far too handsome for her peace of mind. While she stroked her clit with one hand, she picked up the vibrator with the other and rubbed it along the opening of her body. She was wetter than normal so the toy slid in easily.

She shuddered as her need grew stronger. Pushing the head of the vibrator inside, she opened her legs wide. Once the toy was completely lodged to the hilt, she turned it on.

"Ahh!" she cried, the sound too loud in the quiet room. She held her breath for a moment, but the house remained silent.

Sliding the vibrator out, she slowly began to fuck herself, pretending it was Hunter's cock. She alternated between stroking her clit and toying with her nipples, wishing Hunter was with her, sucking on her breasts. She wanted him, wanted to feel him drive into her deep and hard. Her hips began to thrust as she pushed the vibrator in even more.

She groaned again, feeling her climax rise. It hovered at the edges. She was close. So damn close—

There was a quiet knock at her door and it opened immediately.

"Annie? Are you okay?"

She froze mid-stroke as Hunter stood in the doorframe. His gaze saw far too much even before Annie burst into motion. Sitting up, she pulled the vibrator out and grasped the sheet that was pooled at the foot of the bed, dragging it over her naked body.

Hunter didn't move and heat flooded her face. Jesus. He'd caught her red-handed, masturbating. Her humiliation grew when she realized her vibrator was still on, buzzing away on the mattress. She scrambled to find it and turn it off.

He broke the silence first. "I thought you were sick or having a bad dream."

She winced, unable to look him in the face, falling back on the bed with a sigh. She pulled the covers higher, gripping them tightly under her chin. She really wanted to drag them over her head as well. "I'm sorry I woke you. I thought you were still in your office. I'll be quieter. Um… good night."

She expected him to return to his room, but instead he walked toward the bed. God, why couldn't he leave her alone in her mortification? There was no way she could face him after this.

Hunter didn't say anything. The mattress sank and her gaze flew to his face as he lay down beside her. For the first time since he'd come in the room, she actually looked at him. He was wearing nothing but boxer shorts and a bare six-pack that made her drool. He gripped her shoulder and pulled her toward him until they lay on their sides, facing each other. Annie kept the sheet pulled high, while Hunter lay on top of it.

"I didn't mean to interrupt." His mouth was tilted with that gorgeous crooked grin that had gotten her into this mess to begin with.

"What do you think you're doing in my bed?"

"I was having trouble sleeping," he said. "Looks like you were too. Thought maybe we could keep each other company."

"Hunter, I'm not sure—"

"I'm not here to fuck you, Annie. I think maybe we should have a little chat, try to talk our way around what's obviously going to be pretty awkward come morning."

He'd walked in and caught her fucking herself with a vibrator. Awkward didn't begin to cover it.

She grimaced. "Was I that loud?"

Hunter glanced upward at the headboard. "My bed's on the other side of that wall."

Annie sighed. "I didn't realize it was so close. Or that you were in it."

He chuckled. "Obviously."

"God. I'm starting to think that if it weren't for bad luck, I'd have no luck at all. I'm currently holding the world record for dating losers. I travel all the way to Australia to meet a man who's now in New York—the freaking place I just left. My job is on the line thanks to articles I promised to write about the man who is *in New York*. And now this."

Hunter pushed a strand of hair away from her face. Her pussy clenched, her orgasm still hovering, not as close as it was before but not gone. Having Hunter lying next to her on the bed wasn't helping her calm down.

"I don't think you're having bad luck at all."

She narrowed her eyes. "You must be kidding. How can you say that? You know what I've been dealing with."

Hunter shrugged. "I think your luck's been changing lately. Your boss won't give you assignments at work, but then you're handed a big four-part series. You land in Australia all alone and find me."

She snorted. "You think that's good luck, do you?"

Hunter winked. "The best sort. You need a stockman to interview, and you've got me."

"So where's the luck tonight?"

Hunter didn't reply. He didn't need to. His gaze darkened, his jaw hardened. It was a look of pure, unadulterated lust. Her body responded, her embarrassment forgotten in an instant.

Hunter pushed her gently to her back. Her breathing accelerated and her heart pounded so hard it almost hurt. "You said—" she started.

"I meant what I said. I'm not going to fuck you, Annie, but I'm not blind. My timing was about as bad as it can get. I'm going to make up for that." He pulled the sheet away from her body.

She marveled at her stillness, considering how much she wanted this. It took all the strength in her body not to pull him down on top of her. He picked up her vibrator and she blushed once more.

"Open your legs. You're hurting. You need to finish."

She fought to send air to her lungs, but her body wasn't responding. Every nerve, every fiber of her being was focused on him, on what he planned to do. He nudged her thighs apart and slowly slid the vibrator back into her pussy.

She hissed at his too-slow, almost-teasing entry. Her hands balled into fists, gripping the sheet when he lodged the vibrator to the hilt and turned it on once more.

"Hunter." His name came out on a gasp.

"You're the most beautiful woman I've ever met, Annie."

She closed her eyes in pure bliss when he began to thrust the vibrator in and out of her pussy, using her toy with more skill than she'd mastered in years of use. Her body responded, her hips rising for more.

She was close to coming when Hunter's covered erection brushed against her thigh. He was on his side, leaning over her slightly, propped up on his elbow.

She was a greedy bitch, letting Hunter do all the work when he was obviously hurting too. She dragged her hand down his bare chest.

The touch threw off his rhythm and he forgot about the vibrator.

"Annie." His tone was the perfect blend of protest and pleading.

She shushed him. "Let me," she whispered.

She pressed her fingers beneath the waistband of his

boxers and found what she sought. Hunter's cock was rock hard, long and thick. God, her first silly thought when she'd seen him in the airport was that they grew their men big in Australia. She'd had no idea how right she'd been.

Hunter didn't move a muscle as she took a few minutes exploring her new treasure, her fingers tracing his cock—feeling the head, the pulsing vein, the velvety skin. She wrapped her hand around it.

Hunter gripped her hip and turned her back to her side, facing each other once more. He lifted her right leg and put it over his waist. The position made it even easier for her to grip his cock. She tightened her hold and started to stroke his flesh. He groaned his approval before pushing the vibrator back into her pussy, moving it in time with her caresses.

He kissed her softly as they played, neither of them in a hurry to find their release. This moment was too perfect, too good to rush, but soon their bodies made their own demands.

Annie pulled her palm along his dick more roughly. Hunter mimicked, pushing the vibrator inside her quicker, harder. She wished it were Hunter fucking her instead of the toy. But that desire was forgotten when her orgasm came, shaking her frame, her existence. She closed her eyes as she rode out the glorious storm.

She heard Hunter grunt, felt his cock quiver as come spurted from the head, splashing her stomach and the sheet beneath them.

Time passed without recognition as Annie fought to catch her breath, to regain her wits. Which happened all too quickly.

What the hell was that?

Assisted masturbation? With Dylan's brother?

She fought for some sense of regret, of guilt. None

came. Annie felt nothing but exhausted pleasure. "This isn't me. I don't usually do stuff like this."

Hunter kissed the end of her nose. "You're on holiday. People do all sorts of crazy stuff when they're away from home."

Annie gave him a sleepy smile. "So what's your excuse?"

"I was horny." They laughed softly.

"Your bed is sticky," Hunter murmured. Annie could hear the drowsiness in his voice.

"Your fault."

"Nope. Yours. Come on."

She felt him leave the mattress but was too weary to lift her eyelids to see where he was going.

"I'm too tired to move," she complained.

"I know."

"I'll just sleep on the edge of the bed."

Hunter tugged on her arm, lifting her a few inches. "Sleep is what you're going to do, but in my bed."

She tried to respond, but she was drifting too fast, powerless to remain awake. She didn't even comment when Hunter lifted her and carried her to his room.

"Your mum," she said softly.

"Shhh. We'll sort it out in the morning, love. Go to sleep."

Briefly, as she lay next to him, she considered the fact she was naked in Hunter's bed, being spooned by the equally naked, sexy stockman. The night had been sheer magic.

She really had taken a trip to Oz.

HUNTER SLOWLY DISENGAGED from Annie's still body.

Last night, he'd drifted to sleep the instant his head hit the pillow. He wasn't surprised. Annie had rocked his world with just her hand on his cock. She was incredible. His regular morning half-mast hard-on thickened as he considered how much more he wanted to do with the sexy American.

He shook the thought out of his head as soon as it landed. She was here for Dylan. Fuck. His intentions to hold her at arm's length out of respect for his brother had crashed and burned. Hunter pulled on a pair of jeans and glanced at the clock. It was after eight a.m. Typically he was up at dawn, but the late night had apparently taken its toll—on both of them.

Annie didn't stir as Hunter grabbed a t-shirt and shrugged it on. He needed to ring Dylan. He should have gotten his luggage by now. Why wasn't he coming home? Mentally, Hunter did the math and figured out with the time change, his morning was currently his brother's yesterday evening. Jesus. Why couldn't it be the same day and time everywhere?

Hunter walked to the door of his bedroom and opened it. He panicked when he spotted his mum outside Annie's door.

"Hey, Mum. What's up?" Hunter stepped into the hall and closed the door.

Hazel smiled and wished him a good morning. "I thought I'd sneak a peek to see if Annie's still asleep. If not, I'll get breakfast rolling."

"Oh, um…" Hunter needed to stop her. "I haven't heard a sound from her room. I'm sure she's still sleeping."

His mum glanced at the closed door to the guest room. Thank bloody God he'd thought to pull it shut behind him last night. "Maybe you're right. How about you? Ready for something to eat?"

Hunter nodded. "I'm starving." He was. He'd worked up one hell of an appetite.

His mother's grin grew. There was nothing she loved more than feeding her sons. "I'll make you some Vegemite and toast."

She started to walk back down the hall, but turned to say something else. The words died on her lips as Hunter heard his bedroom door open.

Hunter turned and saw Annie standing in the doorframe, wearing one of his t-shirts. Luckily it hung to nearly her knees, but there was no denying she was naked underneath. Her face was flushed and the high color in her cheeks reminded him of her embarrassment last night when he'd walked in on her playing with her vibrator.

God bless her, his mum never missed a beat.

"G'day, Annie. I was about to make breakfast. Are you ready to give the Vegemite another try?"

Annie cleared her throat uncomfortably. "Uh. Sure."

Her agreement proved how uncomfortable she was. She'd sworn to Hunter that hell would freeze over before she'd put that vile stuff in her mouth again.

"I'm sure you'll grow love it," his mum insisted, even though Hunter knew chances were pretty good Annie would hate the black, salty stuff forever. It was definitely an acquired taste, usually one only those born and raised in Australia could stomach. "I'll scramble up a few eggs too. There's no rush, though. Why don't you get a shower and come to the kitchen when you're ready?"

Annie nodded. She looked like a stray cat cornered by a pack of rabid dogs.

His mother continued away from them and neither spoke until they were certain she was out of earshot. Hunter was in for the mother of all Hazel lectures before the day was out, but for now, he was more worried about Annie.

She sighed heavily. "What was that you were saying about my luck getting better?"

Hunter chuckled. "I can't tell if you have bad luck or awful timing."

"God." Annie lightly beat her forehead against the door. "I can't believe your mother watched me walk out of your bedroom in nothing but a t-shirt. *Your* t-shirt, for shit's sake. She must think I'm the biggest slut on the face of the earth."

"Hey now." Hunter pulled her away from the door. "Stop that. Nobody thinks badly of you. Honest. If anything, Mum's probably in the kitchen right now waiting to tear a strip out of my hide for taking advantage of you."

Annie snickered. "Kind of hard to take advantage of the willing."

Her words warmed him. Before he could think better of it, he kissed her. He'd never been much for kissing before, but he'd obviously never met a girl worth the effort. Annie was funny, down-to-earth, adventurous and…fuck a bloody duck, here because Dylan invited her.

Hunter had tried to keep his distance, fight off this attraction between them. That had been a complete failure. Since her arrival at Farpoint, he'd kissed her in the airport, on the couch, by the billabong, then he'd walked into her bedroom last night, joined her in bed and they'd masturbated each other into a couple of mind-blowing orgasms.

So much for his self-restraint.

"Hunter," his mother called out. "Do you mind giving me a hand with something?"

The request was transparent and Annie grinned at him. "Somebody's in trouble," she singsonged.

"I'm thirty years old, Annie. If I want to have a woman in my bed, I can."

"So your girlfriends sleep over all the time?"

The answer to that was simple. He'd never brought a woman back to his bedroom. He was far from a saint, but when he slept with a woman, it was always at her place or in a hotel or, occasionally, he had quickies in the shed. He'd always felt it would be disrespectful to his mother to bring a one-night stand back to the homestead for sex.

That self-proclaimed rule had fallen to the wayside as easily as his determination not to poach on his brother's girl. He was headed straight to hell. And even now, he couldn't make himself give a damn.

"I currently don't have a girlfriend," he responded, dodging her real question.

"Hunter?" his mum yelled again.

"Be there in a minute." Hunter ran his finger along Annie's cheek. "Go get a shower. I'll straighten things out with Mum."

Annie looked uneasy.

"It'll be fine, promise." He sealed his vow with a quick kiss on the cheek. "Oh, and it's going to be hot as blue blazes today, so you'll be fine with a t-shirt, but you might want to consider wearing shorts instead of jeans."

"Okay." Annie walked back into her room.

Hunter girded his loins and headed toward the executioner.

His mum was standing in the foyer. She pointed toward his office and he followed her in silence, shutting the door behind them.

"Listen, before you say anything," he began, "I know I fucked up."

Hazel frowned. "Fucked up how?"

"Annie is here to meet Dylan. She's *his* girl."

Hazel scoffed. "Oh, Hunter. I'm afraid it doesn't work that way. Dylan wrote a few emails to her and they became friends. That doesn't make her 'his'."

"But it was an online dating site and they were obviously interested. They both took off halfway around the world to meet each other."

Hazel crossed her arms. "And who's to say if Dylan had been here, they wouldn't have taken one look at each other and realized it was a mistake?"

"There's no way Dylan won't fall for Annie. She's smart, funny, easy to talk to, sexy."

His mum's smile grew. "Is that right? Well then, by all means, back off until Dylan gets here. Finders keepers and all that jazz."

Hunter recognized his mother's tone. It was one he'd inherited. It was pure, one-hundred-percent sarcasm. "You're pulling my leg, aren't you?"

"Of course I am."

Hunter walked behind his desk and sank into the chair. "So what are you saying? Screw Dylan and go after Annie?"

"Not in so many words. Dylan's in New York. He didn't think twice about heading out of Farpoint to find his destiny, an adventure, maybe even love, and if this doesn't work out for him, I know he'll try again. Because that's Dylan. He's not afraid to seize the day."

Hunter leaned back and studied his mother's face. "Why do I get the feeling I'm going to come out of this conversation looking like a loser?"

Hazel snorted. "Not a loser. Just different. You're so much like your father, Hunter. This property is your life. You're completely committed to your family and to seeing our livelihood succeed. As a result, you won't walk away from your responsibilities here."

"So instead I have to rely on you to fly in prospective brides?"

Hazel rolled her eyes. "I only did that once."

Hunter scoffed. "Six times, mum. You brought six women here."

"I'm your mother. I want you to be happy."

Hunter stood. "I am."

"Are you?"

Her question, spoken quietly, struck a chord. *Was* he happy? Since his father's death, Hunter had moved in a straight line, never straying from the path because his family depended on him to run the business, keep them afloat financially. It was a big job, one that didn't fit between the hours of nine to five. His career was so inter-woven with his life, there wasn't a line where one ended and the other began. Was there a woman in the world who could accept that? Live with that?

A knock at the door saved him from answering.

"Come in," he said.

Keith Munroe, one of the station's best hands, peered around the door. "Bernie's wife went into labor this morn-ing, so the hands are hanging around out there waiting for somebody to give them their list of duties today. Dylan picked a hell of a time to saunter off to America. Any idea when he'll be back?"

Hunter shook his head. Keith had grown up on Farpoint and was close in age to him and Dylan. They'd been best mates as boys and that friendship had never wavered through the years. Though he worked on the station as a jackaroo, Keith wasn't an employee as much as a member of the family.

"Shit." Hunter had known the station foreman's wife was due any day. Figured it would be today, when his mind was on anything but work. "Tell the guys I'll be right there," Hunter replied.

Keith tipped his hat and closed the door. Hunter pointedly tried to ignore the surprise on Hazel's face. When she didn't break the silence, he snapped, "I *do* know what needs to be done around here."

"I didn't say you didn't. It's just been awhile since you've been out there getting your hands dirty. I'm enjoying seeing the jackaroo side of you again."

He shrugged. When Annie told Hazel about her magazine articles, his mother had barely restrained her laughter. Hunter wasn't the stockman Dylan was, but Annie still insisted on shadowing him. He hadn't told Annie the truth about his role on the station originally because he hadn't wanted her to choose someone else to interview. He'd grown up on Farpoint, he and Dylan doing the same chores when they were boys. He was perfectly versed in what it meant to ride herd, raise stock, muster cattle and do head checks. However, with the passing of his father, Hunter had moved away from the life of a jackaroo, opting instead for the desk job.

"I better get out there."

Hazel nodded. "I think you should. I'll send Annie out after she's had some breakfast. She still has those articles to write."

This time his mum didn't bother to hide her matchmaking grin. Hunter had clearly wasted time worrying about her reaction to his interest in Annie. He had her full support. Only problem now was, Hazel would go out of her way to push them together. He really needed to talk to Dylan.

"You won't say anything to embarrass her, will you? Last night was my doing. Not hers. She's worried about what you'll think of her. Maybe it would be good if you let the subject drop completely. Don't mention it."

Hazel threw her hands up, a smile glinting in her eyes. "Since when do I do anything to embarrass anyone?"

Hunter raised a single eyebrow, no less than twenty humiliating instances floating through his memory.

"Oh, go on. Your Annie will be right as rain with me."

Hunter walked toward the shed, grinning despite his anxiety.

Your Annie.

If only she were.

Chapter Six

The sun was just rising as Hunter stood next to Annie, Mutt lounging by her feet lazily. They leaned on the fence, watching Prince and his mother walk around the paddock. After their bumpy start, the little calf's mother soon accepted him and the two had been inseparable. They'd be ready to return to the rest of the herd in a couple more days.

Hunter had been concerned things between he and Annie would be awkward after being caught by his mum yesterday morning, but Annie bounced fast. He assumed years of dealing with unexpected shanghais by the tabloids had thickened her skin in terms of embarrassing easily.

The past two days—like the ones preceding them— had fallen into an easy pattern of chores, meals with his mother and quiet afternoons spent in his office, both of them working on their computers. Annie had sent off her first article after letting him read it. She was an incredibly gifted writer. She'd obviously found her calling as a big city journalist.

Unable to sleep, he'd risen while it was still dark only to

find Annie sitting on the front porch. She'd merely smiled when he joined her. He'd taken her hand and they'd walked in silence, soaking in the last of the cool air. With the sun's arrival, the day would heat up quickly.

"I suppose this cattle station is pretty boring compared to your life in America."

Annie looked at him with wide eyes. "Are you kidding? This place is awesome. I was standing here trying to imagine myself back in New York. I'm not looking forward to the crowds, the noise, the fast pace. Staying here has driven home how crazy my life in the city has gotten. I can't tell you the last time I've noticed the sky or watched a sunrise or taken a deep breath of fresh, clean air. I feel like a prisoner who's been released from jail after years locked away. You're so lucky to be able to call Farpoint home."

Hunter turned to face her. "You're welcome to come back any time you want." Imagining the day when she had to return to her own life left him with a gnawing ache in his gut. He'd woken up every morning since her arrival with a smile on his face, looking forward to the day. He couldn't remember the last time that had been true. He'd fallen into a rut of monotony, forgetting to enjoy the little things—like sunrises, picnics by the lake, the wonder of a newborn calf.

"Thanks, Hunter. You might want to be careful with that invitation though. I'm sure you feel pretty safe offering, thinking I'd never brave another twenty-hour flight, hours spent in that death trap you call a helicopter and even this unbearable summer heat, but I can promise you right now, I would. In a heartbeat."

Hunter brushed a strand of hair from her face and moved closer. He'd wanted to kiss her since yesterday morning, but he'd forced himself to maintain his distance. The tether was stretched too taut. It was about to snap.

"You never told me what your mother said about catching us coming out of your bedroom."

He grinned, surprised Annie hadn't asked him about Hazel earlier. "She was pleased."

"Pleased?"

"She likes you, Annie. A lot. I think there's a part of her that hopes you'll save me from a life of work and one-night stands." He'd meant his words as a joke. Partly.

"Do you want to be saved?"

He'd expected her to latch on to the one-night stand comment. Neither of them had talked much about past relationships. Somehow he knew they didn't matter. What he felt for Annie was different than anything he'd ever experienced with anyone else. She'd alluded to the same. In this relationship, the past didn't exist. It had no significance.

He didn't even need to consider the response to her question. He knew the answer. He leaned forward until their lips were a breath apart. "Only by you."

Annie covered the minute distance separating them, kissing him hard and fast. Hunter took the reins almost immediately. Placing his hands on her hips, he pulled her closer as Annie's arms wrapped around his neck. Kissing her had become as natural as breathing.

They fell into each other. They'd kissed at least half a dozen times since her arrival and yet the overpowering sensation of holding her like this never lessened. The impact was stronger than getting kicked in the gut by a horse. Every time he touched her, the need for more grew.

He broke the kiss, touching his forehead to hers. "I know you Yanks do the whole hayloft thing, but the best I can offer is a shed."

Annie frowned, even as a smile played on her lips. "Shed?"

He grinned. "Wanna make out with me in the shed? There's a stack of hay bales in the corner that almost hits the ceiling."

Annie's smile grew wide. "That sounds…intriguing."

Hunter grasped her hand and tugged her toward the shed. "Just making out, Annie. That's all. I promise. I won't let it go farther than that."

They had less than an hour before the jackaroos started arriving to tackle the day's tasks. Soon the yard would be teeming with men drinking coffee before settling down to work. For now, the station was relatively quiet. He could imagine the satisfied smirk on his mum's face if she were to spot him holding Annie's hand right now. His resolve to keep his hands to himself crumbled even more.

When they entered the shed, he gestured to the hay bales stacked at the back right corner, like a staircase made of tightly compacted straw. Annie started first, climbing each square bale as if she were scaling a mountain. Hunter grabbed a blanket, not waiting for her to reach the top before making his own ascent. He distracted her midway by running his hand down her bare leg. She'd donned shorts again today. They were perfectly appropriate, coming nearly to her knees. Even so, that didn't keep him from fondling her trim calves.

"Keep that up and I'll fall," she chastised, though there was no censure in her voice.

"Don't worry about that. I'd catch you."

She paused for a moment then gave him a sweet smile that knocked the breath from his lungs. What the hell was wrong with American blokes? How could they let a woman like her run around free and lonely for so long?

Once they reached the top of the stack, he resumed the kiss without a word. Annie accepted his embrace, her hands tightening on his waist. Her firm grip told him she was afraid he'd pull away again. He knew he should. Walking away was the right thing to do, but no force of nature was going to stop this stampede. He'd promised her a makeout session and by God, she was getting one.

Hunter tossed his hat to the bale beneath his feet, tangling his fingers in Annie's soft brown hair. She'd joked once that she got all the brains in the family, while her younger two siblings got all the beauty. Hunter couldn't imagine any woman holding a candle to his Annie. Her eyes were bluer than a clear Australian sky. Since arriving in Oz, her porcelain skin had warmed to a beautiful golden brown.

Annie started to sit down, but he stopped her. "Wait." He spread out the large blanket he'd grabbed. "Hay is scratchy stuff. This might help a little."

She helped him pull it over the hay then they lay on their sides, facing each other. "I can't remember the last time I made out on the sly. I feel like a naughty teenager again."

He'd brought loads of girls to the tops of hay bale stacks when he was a boy. He'd learned quite a bit on the hay. "Where did you do your fooling around?"

She grimaced, humor twinkling in her blue eyes. "Oh God. This is sort of embarrassing to admit."

"Tell me."

"The back of my dad's limo."

Hunter shook his head, chuckling. "Jesus. What a life."

She didn't respond. Instead, she ran her hand over his chest, dragging it down until she could slip it under the thin cotton. Then she caressed his bare skin. "If it makes you feel better, I think I prefer it here."

"You think? Sounds like I have my work cut out for me."

He rolled her to her back, moving over her. He'd jerked

off to this image a couple times since her arrival. Annie beneath him, parting her legs to welcome him between.

He pressed his cock against her, enjoying her soft intake of breath. Her face was flushed, her gaze heavy, inviting. She pulled him lower, initiating the next round of kisses. Unlike the hungry ones by the paddock, these were slower, deeper. Their mouths met and fused like time had stopped for them. The sense of urgency dissipated. This was what they were here for. No more. No less. Just this.

He planted soft kisses on her lips, cheeks, neck, even her closed eyelids, and Annie followed suit. He'd never felt such adoration. Neither of them sought to undress or to take the game to the next level. They simply gave and received while holding on tight.

Annie changed the rules first. Her hand left his chest, drifting south until it hovered above his cock. Their eyes met and held. She gave him a sexy grin while trying to unbuckle his belt and open his jeans.

Hunter didn't stop her. Instead, he bent his knees, holding himself up with his hands on the blanket. He wasn't a saint, but above that, he was no fool. He wanted her to touch him. Once she had his pants open, she wasted no time in exposing his cock and gripping it tightly, letting him know she had arrived at her destination.

He hissed between gritted teeth, trying to ignore how fucking good it felt. He was no stranger to fooling around, but in the past, he'd always managed to give as good as he got. Annie's rough rubs against his aching flesh sent him to the top too fast. He needed to get control.

He was about to slow down her sexy pumping when she moved. She shoved against his chest, forcing him away from, then rose on her knees. She pressed him to his back, quickly assuming the top position. Then—holy fuck—she shifted lower.

Hunter closed his eyes, blinded by the stars flashing behind his eyelids as Annie bent down and took him in her mouth.

"Jesus, Annie! So fucking good."

He felt rather than saw her lips curve around the head of his cock. Her grip tightened at the base. He was too large for her to take in all at once, but he'd be damned if she wasn't giving it a try. The head of his dick brushed the back of her throat and he groaned. Annie retreated completely, releasing him with a pop.

Hunter parted his lids, found her looking at him.

"I want you to come in my mouth."

It was all she said before she started to suck his cock back inside.

Hunter swallowed heavily. Fuck. Given the way she was working his erection, he'd say that ending was a foregone conclusion. Worst part was it wasn't going to take long. Hunter started counting heads of cattle in his mind, trying to prolong her sweet torment, but it didn't help.

He reached for her, stroking her hair, whispering words of jumbled nonsense—all his overwrought brain could manage.

"So pretty. God, Annie. Jus' like that. Fuck me. So fucking— *Fuck me.*" Somehow his crazy talk seemed to stoke her own needs. He watched her use her free hand to grasp her breast, pinching the nipple hard.

The added visual fueled his arousal and he was lost. He gripped her face. "Gotta come. Gotta—" They were the only words he managed before his cock erupted. Annie didn't pull away. Instead she took each drop as her reward, swallowing until he was spent.

Hunter's head, which he'd lifted at some point to watch her, fell back against the blanket. Sweat rolled down the side of his face, but he didn't have the strength to wipe it away. His heart pounded so hard he feared it would burst.

Annie moved, coming to lie beside him once more. Hunter turned to face her, gripping her hip and pressing her against his now flaccid cock. He kissed her, long and deep. She'd just rocked his world.

She wiggled against him, trying to find a bit of satisfaction of her own. Hunter broke the kiss, reaching down to unfasten her shorts.

"Hunter," she whispered.

"Shh. Your turn." Annie hadn't bothered removing his pants; instead she'd simply grasped what she wanted. He followed suit.

Pressing his finger against her clit, he marveled at how wet she was. Most women treated blowjobs like a nasty bit of foreplay they merely endured. That didn't appear to be true for Annie. Her nipples were pebbled, poking through her t-shirt, and her cunt was soaking wet and hot as the summer sun. Hunter shoved his entire hand deeper into her shorts, cupping her mound.

Annie moaned, applying her own pressure, pushing against him for more. Curving his hand, he thrust two fingers inside, pumping them fast and deep. Annie responded like a sprinter to a starter gun. Her hips picked up the rhythm of his fingers.

Her eyes drifted closed. Hunter watched a pretty pink hue paint her cheeks. She was a blusher—when embarrassed or hot or in the throes of sex. He'd never thought a mere shade of color could be such a fucking turn-on.

"I want to watch you come."

Tit for tat. Annie had made her request. Now he made his.

She blinked, her gaze finding his for only a moment before her lids closed once more.

"Yes," she whispered. Then, like him, her words were jarred loose. Driven by pure lust and need, she seemed to disengage, releasing control of her thoughts, just as his had. Annie was his kind of lover. Her dirty demands were the stuff of his wet dreams.

"Harder! God, Hunter. Go faster. I need…deep. Three."

He added another finger, stretching her tight pussy even more. Annie liked it rough. Christ. So did he. Her body stiffened only a second before her muscles clenched against him. He didn't let up, didn't cease until he'd wrung every beautiful spasm, shiver and shudder out of her.

Only when her climax subsided did he soften his thrusts. Slowly, he dragged his fingers out. Annie didn't move for several moments, giving Hunter time to study her pretty face. When she'd first arrived, she'd been pale, with dark circles under her eyes. He'd blamed travel for that tiredness, but after hearing about her life in New York, he suspected perhaps that was her natural state. As the days passed, he'd watched the tension around her eyes and mouth lessen. Her skin had darkened with the sun, a few cute freckles appearing on her nose and cheeks.

Right now, as she lay boneless, replete, she looked healthy, relaxed. Beautiful.

Finally Annie's eyes opened, her gaze finding his. Neither of them spoke as she rolled to face him. He was reminded of lying with her like this in his bed as she stroked his cock. It was a new position for him, but it was suddenly his favorite. Lying close to her, watching her expressive blue eyes, sharing her air, knowing he could reach out and touch her anywhere, at anytime. It was as close to heaven as he'd ever come.

"Thank you," she whispered after several silent moments.

His mouth twisted into a crooked grin and he wiggled his eyebrows. "For what?"

She narrowed her eyes. "Well, for that," she gestured to her lower body, "but also for the last few days. I'd sort of hit a wall at home. Hit a point where I just couldn't take one more step. I feel stronger now."

He kissed the tip of her nose. "I'm glad."

"Did you know yesterday was Thanksgiving? Or, well...*today*. God. The stupid time difference is so confusing."

He shook his head. "That's one of your American holidays, right?"

She nodded. "Yep. Usually families get together for a big meal and to take a moment to say what they're thankful for."

He frowned. "Shouldn't you be home with them?"

She sighed and closed her eyes. "I love my family, Hunter. I truly do. My sisters sort of drive me nuts, but they're funny and harmless most of the time. They're twins too. Did I tell you that?"

"No. I didn't know that."

"I'm older by four years."

Hunter did the math. Annie, at seven, would have remembered their mother leaving, however, her younger sisters had only been three. They'd never known what it was like having a mother in the house. Annie did.

"My father's wealth increased as we got older and with that money came more and more exposure."

"I thought you said your father sort of promoted that."

Annie's lips tightened. She'd been so relaxed just a few minutes ago. Hunter hated to see that easiness go away. "He did. Apparently there's a gene in my family that makes them crave attention. It's dominant in my dad and sisters, recessive in me and my mom."

Suddenly things were making more sense. The one person who'd grounded Annie, made her feel secure in her family, in her own skin, had left her alone to deal with those differences.

"Is that why she left? The attention?" he asked.

Annie nodded slowly. "Yeah. I think so." She paused. "I know so. The tabloids drove her nuts. Do you know where she is now?"

Hunter shook his head.

"In a little villa in Tuscany. The place is completely isolated except for a few neighboring villagers."

"Does she still live with her younger man?"

"Yeah. They've been married for nearly twenty years. He works in a vineyard and she putters in the garden and writes poetry. They don't travel often because my mom says she's never found anywhere as beautiful as Italy, anywhere that brings her that same peaceful feeling. I've visited her a few times. It's nice, don't get me wrong, but I don't get that same sense of home there that she does."

Hunter could appreciate that idea. He'd never left Australia and had only traveled to Sydney and Adelaide a handful of times. While it had been cool to see the lights of the bigger cities, he'd missed home. Farpoint held his heart and always would. It seemed Annie was still searching for her place in the world.

"Are you happy in New York, Annie?"

Her response came instantly. "No. Not really."

"Then why are you there?"

This time her answer took longer. He could see her formulating her response, searching for the right words. "Honestly? I have no idea. I think I settled there after college because that's where my family was, because that's where the jobs were. Before I knew it, one day had become a month and a month had become a year, then six years had passed. I kept going because it was easier than uprooting, moving somewhere else."

"Why did you come to Australia?"

"Because I'm tired of playing it safe. Tired of accepting the status quo. I want my home, Hunter. It's out there. And I'm going to find it."

It was on the edge of his lips to tell her to stay longer, to try Farpoint on for size. Ridiculous as it seemed given her short stay, Hunter suspected Annie belonged here. Unfortunately, he couldn't extend that offer. Not until he cleared things with Dylan.

He'd put off talking to his brother for days, uncertain what to say. Now he knew. He wanted Annie. Somehow he'd have to make Dylan understand.

A car door slamming outside the shed recalled them to their present state.

Hunter rose slowly, hooking his pants back up. "I suppose we should head to the house. The work day is about to start."

Annie set herself to rights as well then took his proffered hand and they descended the hay bale staircase.

When they returned to the house, they ran into Hazel at the front door, carrying a small overnight bag.

"Running away from home?" Hunter teased.

"It's my turn to stay with your Aunt Joyce. She had her hip replacement surgery. I told you about it a few days ago."

Everything had been a whirlwind since Annie's arrival. So much so, he'd forgotten his mother had promised to take a turn caring for his elderly great aunt. "Oh yeah. That's today?"

Hazel nodded slowly. "And tonight. I'm sleeping there as well." Her gaze traveled from his face to Annie's. Damn observant woman.

Annie must have felt the penetrating look as well. "I think I might head upstairs for a quick shower," she said.

Hunter didn't want to let her go, but Hazel clearly had some piece to speak and he wasn't going to be given an easy escape like Annie.

"Of course, dear." Hazel gave her a motherly kiss on the cheek. Annie smiled at the gesture and, for a moment, Hunter thought he saw the sheen of tears. "You have a nice day and I'll see you tomorrow afternoon."

Annie said goodbye to his mum. Hunter watched her walk down the hallway, knowing he was in a whole world of trouble—and not with his mother.

He was falling in love with Annie Prince.

Hunter Sullivan, the world's most practical man, was losing his heart to a woman who didn't even live on the same continent, whose father had more money than God, who had come here because of her interest in Dylan. Fuck.

"Call Dylan."

Hunter glanced at his mum, trying to ignore the elephant in the room. "You need a hand with your bag?"

Hazel narrowed her eyes. "No. I don't."

"How about I drive you over there?"

She shook her head. "Keith's waiting in the truck. He'll take me. Call your brother."

"I will, Mum."

His mother reached over and placed her hand on his shoulder. "If for no other reason, Hunter, than to tell him how you're feeling."

He nodded. His mother left and Hunter watched the retreating truck until the taillights disappeared into the darkness.

Then he walked over to the phone. It rang the moment he touched the receiver.

He answered with his usual. "G'day."

"Hunter."

A twin moment. It wasn't the first time he and Dylan had reached out to find each other at exactly the same moment. His mother always laughed and it was she who'd dubbed them "twin moments".

Hunter forced a casual tone to his voice. "Dylan. How you goin'?"

"I'm doin' all right. Mum says you've been entertaining Annie there for me. Well done, mate."

"Are you on your way home?"

It took a few seconds for Dylan to reply. "No."

"You still missing your luggage?"

Dylan cleared his throat. "Uh, no. I got it back a couple hours ago. Just thinking I might stay here a little longer."

"You're going to stay in New York? I didn't think you were interested in sightseeing. Thought you were just going to meet Annie."

"Yeah. I was, but I met Annie's friend, Monet. She's been putting me up, showing me around. Is, uh, Annie planning on coming back soon?"

Dylan was still expecting to see Annie. "Didn't Mum tell you? Annie's staying here for a couple weeks. She's writing an article about the cattle station for her magazine."

"Oh yeah. Monet said she'd gotten an assignment. Didn't think she'd do it with me here."

Hunter heard music in the background, heard Dylan say something to someone else.

"Where are you?" Hunter asked.

"I'm at Monet's. We're about to start making Thanksgiving dinner. We just got home from a parade. Give me a minute, Monnie. I'm going to take this call in the other room."

Hunter couldn't miss the peculiar tone in Dylan's voice. Something seemed odd, but he couldn't put his finger on what it was. It was throwing Hunter off, making it harder for him to confess what he was feeling for Annie. If Dylan was having problems in New York, Hunter didn't want to add to his misery.

"I'm alone now," Dylan said after a few moments.

"Dylan, are you okay?"

"Yeah, I'm fine. I just… Ah, fuck a bloody duck. I'm just going to say it. Call me a dickhead all you like, but I think I've fallen arse over tit for Monet. I feel like shit, given that Annie flew all the way to—"

"Jesus, Dylan," Hunter interrupted, the breath flying out of him in a relieved swoosh.

"I know, man. I fucked up. Big-time."

"No," Hunter said. "You didn't. I think I'm already halfway in love with Annie."

"You are?"

"And I've been feeling like a right prick for stealing your girl."

Dylan's laugh washed over him like rain on a hot summer day. Calmness descended on Hunter. He realized it was the first time since Annie arrived and turned his world on its ear that he didn't have an ache in his chest.

"Didn't expect *that*. Sorta figured you'd chew my arse off and tell me to get my shit together and hop on the next plane."

Hell no. "I think you should stay in New York. See what's what with this new girl. Give it a chance. She could be your soul mate."

Hunter could hear the shock in Dylan's voice. "Is this the same brother who told me to get my head out of my arse? Told me flying to New York was the dumbest thing I've ever done in my life?"

"One and the same. You can kick *my* arse for being a self-righteous prick when you get home."

Dylan's sigh of relief traveled all the way to Farpoint. "Deal."

Hunter heard a female voice before Dylan said, "I need to go. Give Mum and Annie my love."

"Will do."

The phone clicked off before Hunter could say goodbye.

Dylan was staying in the States. He'd met another woman.

Hunter's smile grew.

This changed everything.

Chapter Seven

Annie turned off the shower and sighed. After her heated interlude with Hunter in the shed, she'd felt the need for distance to gather her thoughts. It had taken every ounce of strength in her body not to insist that he fuck her right there in the hay. Unfortunately, he'd made it perfectly clear on several occasions that he wouldn't let things go too far because of Dylan.

The truth was, months of emails and Skyping with Dylan had never left her feeling the way she'd felt as she lay next to Hunter just talking. It was becoming abundantly clear that even if she and Dylan hadn't crossed wires, they would never have produced the same sparks or shared the undeniable chemistry she had with Hunter.

She'd thought taking a shower would clear her mind, but it hadn't. The only problem it had alleviated was the itchiness. Hunter hadn't lied. Hay was scratchy stuff.

She pulled back the shower curtain and grabbed a towel from the rack. As she did so, a huge spider dropped to the floor and scurried through the door to her bedroom.

Annie cringed then panicked. Quickly wrapping the

towel around her, she darted from the bathroom to her bedroom door, keeping a very close watch on the floor.

Dashing out into the hallway, she ran straight into Hunter.

Her face must have betrayed her fear. "Annie. What's wrong?"

"Spider. In there," she gasped. "You have to kill it."

She'd expected him to rush to her rescue, but instead, an amused grin covered his face. "What kind of spider?"

She scowled. "A fucking big-ass spider! Go find it and kill it."

Hunter rubbed his face but the movement didn't fool her. He was trying to hide the fact he was laughing.

"Hunter. I can't sleep in there until I know that thing is dead. What if it crept under the sheets?" She shivered at the thought and realized regardless of the spider's imminent death, she was facing a few rough nights, imagining bugs crawling all over her. She hated spiders.

Her complaint didn't trigger the same disgust in Hunter. Instead, the twinkle in his eyes faded and morphed into something much more thrilling as his gaze drifted lower, studying her dripping hair and body. "I have a better idea."

He didn't bother to explain. He didn't need to when he grasped her hand and led her to his bedroom. "I think you should start spending your nights—and even some of your days—in *my* bed."

Her heart slammed into her throat. He couldn't possibly be offering the invitation she was hoping for. Could he? "And where will you be?"

"Beside you. The only thing crawling over your body tonight is going to be me."

"But I thought—"

"I spoke to Dylan on the phone. Explained things."

Annie narrowed her eyes, confused. "I see. So why don't you explain some of those *things* to me too."

Hunter pulled her into his room and shut the door. He pressed her against it, his body so close, the chill she'd felt since leaving the shower disappeared completely.

"You may have come here for Dylan, Annie, but if you leave, it'll be as *my* girl."

Too many words resonated in her brain.

If you leave.

My girl.

She wasn't sure how to respond, but it didn't matter. Hunter clearly wasn't expecting an answer.

He backed off, his gaze dropping to the towel she was still clutching around her. "You're wet."

She nodded stupidly, afraid to speak, to break the spell. Hunter wanted her. His reservations had disappeared, replaced by sheer, unadulterated lust…and need.

He lightly pulled her hands away from the towel where she held it in place, then gripped the cotton and dragged it from her body.

She forgot to breathe as the soft material stroked her damp skin in its retreat. Then Hunter had the towel hanging loose in his grip as she stood naked before him. He'd seen her in various states of undress over the past few days, but never like this, never totally nude in a well-lit room, standing in front of him. Her nakedness was made more thrilling by the fact he was still fully dressed.

She was on fire. How could he make her feel this way so quickly?

"You're stunning," he whispered.

She felt the flush creep to her cheeks, but it wasn't humiliation fueling the fire. It was nothing short of all-out, balls-to-the-wall need. "I want you. So badly."

His gaze snapped to hers as she spoke. "Jesus, Annie. I

want to do this right, but I think I could come just from looking at you."

She smiled. "Seems to me like we have all day…and night."

Hunter growled. An honest-to-God growl. Her body responded as if she were a bitch in heat. Her nipples pebbled and her pussy grew even wetter. "*Every* night. Every night you're here, I want you in my bed."

Once again his words reminded her that this visit was only temporary. She was setting herself up for the heartbreak of the century. Hunter lifted the towel and slowly used it to wipe away the drops of water on her overheated skin. Fuck it. She was tired of measuring each move, watching her step out of fear. She wanted Hunter. She'd deal with the rest later.

Each rub of the towel made her breath catch, her heart race, her pussy clench with desire.

She went lightheaded when he dropped to his knees, continuing his gentle caresses over her hips, down her legs, even paying attention to her feet. When he started back up, the towel stroking the inside of her legs, she parted them, willing him to come closer.

He stopped when he reached the juncture of her thighs. Looking down, she caught his wicked smile. He dropped the towel, his fingers lightly touching her opening. "You're staying wet here. All day if I can manage it."

She thrilled at his dirty talk. "All night too?" Her tone was infused with a dare, but also hope.

He chuckled. "I'll do my best, love." He leaned closer and slowly swiped his tongue along her slit. She shivered, her head falling against the door. Hunter pushed her legs farther apart, his tongue stroking her clit, the opening to her pussy. When he lifted one of her legs, placing her knee on his shoulder so he could reach even deeper, she closed her eyes and tried to fight off her orgasm.

Her palms flattened against the door as Hunter nipped at her clit, his teeth producing a sharp, pleasurable sting that he quickly soothed with a soft kiss. For several minutes, he teased her flesh with tiny pains and delicate strokes, every move he made driving her closer to that gorgeous crossroads of lust and insanity.

When he thrust his tongue inside her, she was a goner. She fisted her hands in his hair and cried out his name. Hunter responded—not with words, but actions. His tongue went deeper, faster. She loved it, but knew she wanted so much more. She wouldn't rest until it was his cock driving her to madness.

Hunter gripped her ass, squeezing the globes tightly, using them as leverage to hold her pussy to his questing tongue. When his fingers slipped deeper into the crack, the tip of one digit grazing her anus, she exploded. Her body quivered as tiny electrical sparks flashed inside her. Holy mother. Everything he did felt so fucking good.

When Annie's wits returned, she found herself on her back in the middle of Hunter's bed. He stood watching her, slowly removing his clothes. She wanted to help, wanted to participate in baring his body, but her limbs wouldn't cooperate. She felt as weak as a newborn kitten.

Hunter didn't seem to mind. His dimples appeared at her soft intake of breath as he pulled off his shirt and his jeans. She'd discovered in the shed that her Aussie cowboy went commando. She'd touched his cock, held it in her mouth, but even after all that, the image of it as he stood before her now took her breath away. Her pussy clenched as she imagined him pushing all that thickness inside her.

Once he was naked and she'd looked her fill, she lifted her hand, inviting him to join her on the bed.

Hunter crawled onto the mattress, not stopping until he straddled her legs, hovering above her. She was a captured animal to his steely cage. She never wanted to be set free.

Hunter slowly lowered his body. While he supported most of his own weight with his arms, he made certain they were connected, skin to skin, from chest to toes.

Then he kissed her.

The way Hunter kissed could be declared a freaking Olympic event. He took the melding of lips and tongues and teeth and turned it into something truly inspirational.

Unable to resist, Annie ran her fingers through his dark honey-blond hair. Hunter cupped her cheek with one hand and she swooned a bit. She loved the way his large hand cradled her face, making her feel cherished, special.

Soon, kissing gave way to more touching as she lightly scratched Hunter's muscular back, letting him feel the sting of her nails. He fielded her hit and lobbed one of his own, bending his head to suck one of her nipples into his mouth, increasing the pressure until she squealed.

He offered no reprieve. Instead, he turned his head and issued the same sweet torture to her other breast.

She lifted her legs and locked them tightly around his waist. His cock nestled near the opening to her body, pressed lengthwise along her slit. He was hot and hard and she was so, so ready.

Hunter continued to play with her breasts, alternating sucks, licks and bites until she was squirming mindlessly beneath him.

"Please," she whispered.

Hunter didn't respond, didn't appear to have heard.

She repeated her plea louder, then louder again. Hunter ignored her. She threw her head against the pillow in frustration. "God, Hunter! *Please*," she yelled.

He lifted his head and waited until she looked at him. "You can beg all you want, love, but I promised you all day. I don't make promises lightly."

"But it hurts!"

Hunter frowned, concern covering his handsome features. How was it fair to women everywhere to have this perfectly formed man walking around loose? "Bad hurt?" he asked.

"Horny hurt."

Hunter chuckled. It was the wrong response, given her state. She punched his shoulder, his arm. Striking against her stockman was as effective as trying to knock down a skyscraper with a pillow.

"Want to play rough?" She heard the teasing note in his voice—just before he tickled her.

She was extremely ticklish. She wiggled, trying desperately to escape his wicked fingers as she laughed uncontrollably. "Stop!" Her request came between giggles that simply dared Hunter to up his game. She twisted to her stomach, trying to crawl away from him.

"Hey," he protested, covering her back with his chest, using his weight to pin her beneath him. His breath was hot against her ear, his lips touching the back of her neck. "No escape." If he meant his words as a threat, he'd missed the mark. Once again he'd trapped her and she didn't give a shit.

"You remind me of a brumby we owned once."

"What's a brumby?" she asked.

"A horse. Willful, untamed. Glorious. Like you. It took a bit of doing, but I finally managed to control her."

She looked over her shoulder. "How?"

Hunter's gaze darkened with unsuppressed lust. "I tied her up."

Annie shivered and Hunter cursed.

"Fuck, Annie. It's our first time together. I want to make love to you. Treat you sweet, like you deserve. Now you've got me thinking about stuff…"

"What stuff?"

He shook his head. Hunter was a gentleman. Of that, she had no doubt. She also recognized the wilder side hidden beneath the surface. She'd spent years in a vanilla world, accepting missionary position as her fate, never finding a man who'd earned her trust the way Hunter had.

But there was a difference between acceptance and defeat. Deep within, she'd never let go of the hope she'd find a man who would let her explore her sexual boundaries. Her heart told her Hunter was that man.

"Would you tie me up?"

Hunter closed his eyes, but his stuttered breathing prompted her to keep pushing.

"Would you take me over your knee and spank me?"

"Bloody hell. Don't do this, love. I'm barely holding on as it is."

She pushed her ass against his thick cock, shoving it deeper within the crack. "What if I asked for those things? Would you give them to me?"

Silence was her answer. Annie counted ten heartbeats and then Hunter's patience broke. He rose from the bed and panic besieged her. Had she read him completely wrong? Disgusted him with her secret wants?

She started to lift up, but Hunter halted her. "Don't." His voice was deep, strong. "Don't move a muscle."

While he didn't add a threat to his command, his tone certainly implied there would be a punishment. Annie sank onto her stomach and looked over her shoulder in time to see Hunter returning to the bed with a tie.

"Didn't picture you as the dress-up type." Was that sultry voice really coming from her?

Hunter didn't respond. Instead, he knelt next to her on the mattress. "Put your hands above your head."

Annie complied as Hunter quickly and efficiently tied her wrists together before binding them to the headboard. Oh yeah. There were definite advantages to hooking up with a cowboy. She didn't have more than a second to test the bondage and realize she was well and truly stuck before he issued his next command.

"Get on your knees. Arse in the air."

Annie assumed the position quickly. The flames Hunter lit inside her exploded into an inferno as she found herself in the midst of one of her favorite fantasies. Truth wasn't just stranger than fiction. It was fucking better too. Way better.

Hunter pushed her knees apart and claimed the spot between her legs. She flushed when she realized the bird's-eye view he was getting of all her girlie bits. He gripped her ass cheeks, separating them, opening her even more to his perusal.

She may be a liberated, independent woman, but she couldn't deny how much she loved being under Hunter's control in bed. His hands tightened on her flesh. She wriggled with need.

"Shhh," he whispered. "You're so wet, Annie. Your thighs are shiny, slick." To prove his words true, he ran his fingers through her juices. She shivered. Everything he said and did drove her closer to an edge she'd never reached before.

She wanted so much from him, her voice failed her. What would she ask for? His fingers? His mouth? His cock? She wanted it all.

Hunter made the decision for her as he pressed two fingers inside her pussy, thrusting lightly at first, then building speed. She trembled, recalling the strength of her orgasm in the hay. Hunter had taken her there with just those magic fingers of his.

Her hands fisted, the sensation of the ties at her wrists ramping her arousal even more.

Somewhere along the line, he'd added a third finger, stretching her even tighter. She knew the snugness she felt now wouldn't even compare to how taut she'd be when he filled her with his cock. Her hips answered his hand, each entrance met with more pressure as she pushed against him. She'd nearly reached the pinnacle when Hunter retreated.

She groaned. "Don't stop."

He didn't answer. His fingers touched her ass again and she sighed with relief. He was coming back…

Only he didn't. Not exactly. His wet fingers didn't take her pussy. Instead, he used her body's moisture somewhere else. The tip of his finger grazed her anus. When he'd touched her there earlier, she'd been shocked by the impulses it fired inside her.

"Hunter?"

"Just exploring, Annie. For now. I told you before. You make me want too many things. Not all of them are going to be nice or easy. Have you ever—"

"No," she answered quickly. As soon as the word flew from her mouth, she regretted it, curious now about what he'd wanted to ask. Had she ever what? Had a finger there? A cock? A toy? It didn't matter. The answer to all of the above was still no. But now she was left wondering where his thoughts were taking him.

Hunter bent over her back and placed a soft kiss on her cheek. The sweet gesture was in direct contrast to his next words.

"I'm going to fill that pretty arse of yours with lube and fuck it."

She swallowed heavily.

"Would you let me do that, Annie?"

She nodded, her throat too clogged to speak.

He kissed her again. "God, I love you."

The words had come easily, blending in with the moment as Hunter returned to kneeling between her legs. She wasn't even sure he knew what he'd said, but that didn't stop the words from shaking Annie to the core.

The sound of a condom wrapper crinkling distracted her. Then she felt the head of Hunter's cock as it pressed into her pussy. She'd been right. His fingers hadn't even begun to stretch her as much as his huge erection was. She hissed, breathing through her mouth as she tried to assimilate her body to his gorgeous invasion.

Hunter sensed her discomfort, slowing his entrance. His fingers drifted around her waist, playing with her clit until more moisture filled her pussy, allowing him to burrow deeper. He played her body to perfection, using his touches on her clit, his sweet words, his soft kisses along her spine to turn her to pure, molten jelly. Once he'd lodged himself fully inside her, he stopped moving.

"Okay?"

She nodded. Then shook her head. Tears sprang to her eyes. She tried to hide them but Hunter was too observant.

"Hey." He leaned over her body. "Am I hurting you?"

"No. I just…"

What the hell could she say? She'd just realized she'd fallen head over heels in love with him. Not a crush or infatuation. Not mild attraction or lust. She was fucking heart-thumping, sweaty palms, pulsing cunt in love with Hunter Sullivan. A stockman from Australia. What the fuck was she supposed to do with that?

Rather than speak what was in her heart, she lied. Sort of.

"You feel so good inside me. Would you…I mean, could you fuck me hard? *Really* hard?"

In her fantasies, she'd dreamed of being tied down, taken from behind. He'd brought her this far. There was no going back now. She needed him. Wanted him. She'd take her shattered heart back to New York and count the pain well worth it if only he'd finish what they'd started.

Hunter pushed back to his knees and took her farther than she'd ever dared to go in her dreams. Each pounding entry shook her frame, each sliding retreat an agony as she waited for his return. He thrust inside her harder and deeper, the pressure building until she screamed her release.

He didn't stop, didn't offer a reprieve. He pummeled faster, hitting places that had never known the touch of a man. Her second orgasm came quicker, rattling her bones, causing her teeth to chatter.

Hunter froze as she came. He hadn't shared her release. While her hazy brain knew he'd held back, she couldn't formulate the question to ask why.

She collapsed to her stomach, the motion pulling her away from Hunter's still-hard cock. Reaching up, he released her hands from the tie, helping her pull them down to her sides. He gently massaged her shoulders and she groaned as he eased the muscles until the pins and needles prickling in her hands subsided.

He slowly turned her onto her back. She cupped his dear, beloved cheek and smiled.

"Was it everything you wanted?" he asked.

"And more," she whispered. Her voice was hoarse from screaming. Thank God his mother had gone away. Otherwise she would have beat down the door, thinking Annie was being murdered.

"My turn." He nudged her legs apart once more. "My way."

She remembered his desire to make love to her. He slowly pushed his cock back into her body. Once he was seated to the hilt, he kissed her. Deep, drugging, soul-stealing kisses.

Her subconscious mind had convinced her to ask for the dirty fantasy. Had she really thought the request for rough sex would protect her from this? She'd thought the bondage, the hard claiming would keep her heart safe. She'd been a fool.

Hunter could have insisted on complete celibacy and she'd still be right here. Looking into the bright green eyes of the only man she'd ever loved.

He must have noticed something change in her face. What did he see? Sadness, fear, excitement, joy? They were all there.

He gave her one more quick kiss. "It'll be all right, Annie."

The words soaked into her skin like a balm. She nodded. Then she gave herself up to his embrace, the moment, as he slowly made love to her.

When her climax came again, Hunter was with her. And when he pulled her into his arms, spooning her as they drifted off to nap, it was his last words that granted her peace.

It'll be all right.

Chapter Eight

Annie sat behind the wheel of Hunter's ute. She'd parked at the edge of the landing pad as Hunter expertly brought the helicopter to rest in the field.

Dylan was home.

He'd called out of the blue twenty-four hours earlier to say he was coming back to Farpoint. Annie wasn't sure what had happened between him and Monet, but his hasty return indicated it hadn't ended well.

Since making love to her, Hunter had taken their relationship from zero to sixty. He'd made her breakfast in bed, placing a bunch of acacia, what he called "wattle", in a vase on the tray. Yesterday he took her for another picnic by the billabong. This time, she'd accepted his invitation to skinny dip and they'd had sex in the cool water—twice.

Hazel had decided to stay with Aunt Joyce for a couple of days, only returning earlier this morning. Annie wasn't sure if Hunter had asked his mother to stay away or if the woman had a sixth sense about their budding relationship. Either answer was completely plausible.

Hunter had invited her to come with him to pick up

Dylan at Sydney International, but Annie wasn't willing to depart Eden, not even for a few hours. She'd gotten spoiled by the absence of paparazzi. She'd turned him down, more than happy to use her fear of flying as the excuse.

She rubbed her palms against her jeans nervously. Hunter said he'd explained things to his brother. In their haste to get into each other's pants, Annie had failed to nail down exactly what those things were. What had Hunter said? That they were dating? Fucking? Friends with benefits?

Regardless of Hunter's romantic gestures, neither of them had ventured into the *feelings* realm and, because of that, Annie had dismissed his declaration of love the other night as a slip of the tongue. It was a common enough thing to say when in the midst of sex.

She suddenly wished she and Hunter had talked about what was happening between them. It would be a difficult discussion on its own, but with Dylan at the station, it would be even more awkward.

She watched the propellers slow to a stop then Hunter climbed out. Her breath caught. He'd only been gone ten hours and yet, she'd missed him terribly. She stepped out of the ute and waved, smiling from ear to ear. He looked good enough to eat. She started to walk toward him, but stopped as Dylan came around the helicopter.

Mutt, spotting his owner, leapt out of the truck bed and ran over to Dylan, barking loudly. Dylan stopped to pet the dog. Annie wondered how he managed to stay upright when the huge dog jumped up, placing his enormous paws against Dylan's chest. Dylan laughed as he rubbed the dog's ears affectionately.

Hunter made a comment she was too far away to hear and Dylan laughed. She knew they were identical, but seeing them side-by-side drove home just how much so.

Both men looked at her as they crossed the field.

She and Dylan stared at each other for a moment before she broke the silence. "Hi, Dylan."

"Annie?"

She nodded. No doubt he'd expected to glimpse the American girl he'd seen through Skype. In one short week, that pale woman had disappeared, replaced by the tan one standing before him in tatty jeans and boots, an Akubra on her head. Her nervousness grew worse. Hunter, God bless him, must have noticed. He stepped away from Dylan, closer to her. She struggled to read the look on his face, and again she was struck by the likeness between him and Dylan.

"You look like your brother."

Dylan grinned. "Nah, I'm the good-looking one."

Annie smiled. The response was so typically Dylan. The Dylan she'd come to know and consider a friend.

Hunter rolled his eyes and muttered, "idiot," but there was no malice in his voice. In fact, Annie could sense the affection, the love they shared for each other.

"So, you and Hunter, eh?"

Leave it to Dylan to take the bull by the horns.

She nodded slowly, wondering if that was the right reply.

Dylan's green eyes radiated warmth and affection, but none of the lust Annie had grown used to seeing in Hunter's. "Well, I suppose we better go ahead and make sure fate was right."

Annie frowned, confused. But Dylan didn't give her a chance to question him.

He placed his palms on each side of her face and pulled her toward him for a kiss.

Shock held her still for three heartbeats, four, and then she joined the experiment. She softened her lips and let

Dylan lead the kiss. She tried—really tried—but after several seconds, her suspicions were confirmed. Dylan appeared to come to the same conclusion as well. He released her.

"Had your fun?" Hunter's voice held a tinge of annoyance, maybe even a bit of fear, but no real anger.

Dylan's easy smile returned. "Bit like I imagine kissing Linda would be," he said to Hunter. Glancing back at Annie, he explained, "A cousin from Perth we rarely see."

As easily as that, the ice was broken. Annie gave Dylan a friendly hug that he returned. He even picked her up and spun her around a couple times.

"Damn, it's good to finally meet you, Annie. Has my brother been taking good care of you?"

She blushed before she could stop herself and Dylan laughed loudly. "I'll take that as a yes."

Hunter tugged Annie away from Dylan's embrace, wrapping his arm around her shoulders in a sweetly possessive gesture. "We weren't expecting you home so soon. Sort of got the feeling you were taking a fancy to New York."

Annie couldn't imagine Dylan actually enjoying city life. Every time she'd tried to picture Hunter traveling to New York, she realized it would be like placing a wild stallion in a pen, never allowing it to run free. That unnerving thought had woken her up from a sound sleep the previous night. Her first week in Farpoint had passed far too quickly. This time next week she'd be the one standing near the helicopter, preparing to return to the States or—as she'd come to think of it—hell.

"New York was all right."

"And you met Monet?" Of all the people Annie had left behind, Monet was the one she missed the most.

Dylan nodded, his easy smile fading a bit. It confirmed

Annie's fears. Whatever had occurred between her best friend and Hunter's brother, it hadn't ended well. "I did."

He didn't offer more. Annie looked at Hunter, but his expression proved he was just as in the dark as she.

"I guess we better get you back to the house before Mum stomps out here on her own to see you."

Dylan quickly accepted his brother's reprieve. "Much as it pains me to say, I actually missed the old duck."

He slung his pack over his shoulder and headed for the pickup truck, climbing into the bed with Mutt.

Annie looked toward Hunter for an explanation, but he merely shrugged. "Whatever happened, he's not talking."

"Maybe he just needs time."

Hunter nodded, grasping her hand and leading her to the truck. His expression told her he didn't believe time would help Dylan any more than she did.

———

FIVE DAYS PASSED and Dylan still wouldn't talk about his hasty departure from New York. Annie stopped pressing for details as other anxieties began to creep up on her. She was scheduled to return to New York the day after tomorrow.

Annie lay staring at the ceiling of Hunter's bedroom, listening to his soft breathing while fighting off a growing panic attack.

Her Scarlett O'Hara approach to her relationship with Hunter had been a huge mistake. She was running out of tomorrows.

"I thought *I* was the early riser."

She glanced to her left to find Hunter awake and looking at her.

"Trouble sleeping?"

She nodded. "I leave soon." For days, she'd fought against announcing the obvious. Their days had fallen into an easy routine that Annie was too willing to cling to. She'd been pretending her time here was reality. She couldn't live that lie anymore.

Hunter sighed. "I know. It's been on my mind pretty much twenty-four-seven since you got here."

"Really?" He'd never mentioned it, never let on he was bothered by her imminent departure. Maybe she wasn't the only one trying to stop time by living in fantasyland.

He reached over, pulling her to her side, facing him. It was a position she was becoming addicted to. He kissed her softly. "Of course I have."

He would have said more. She knew he was willing to talk it out with her, but once again, her fear kicked in, overwhelming her common sense. She lifted her leg around his waist, grinding her pelvis against his erection. Hunter had teased her last night, claimed she was insatiable. She'd taken it as a compliment, pushing him to his back and riding him in true jillaroo fashion.

She tried to kiss him, but Hunter held her back, his hand on her cheek. "Annie, don't you think we should—"

"No," she interrupted. "Not now. Not yet. I can't...I want..."

Hunter had become adept at reading her face, her emotions. She couldn't remember there ever being another living soul who was so in tune with what she was feeling.

He let her kill the conversation with kisses, touches. They slept naked, neither of them wanting even the thin cotton of a t-shirt between them at night. Hunter pushed her to her back and entered her in one smooth, well-practiced thrust. They'd dispensed with condoms that day by the billabong when Hunter had taken her in the water.

His kisses grew harder and she sensed the desperation

behind them. She felt it. Shared the same fear. She gripped his hair, fisted it tightly. Hunter hissed but didn't break away. Reaching up, he took her hair as well, mimicking her actions, pulling on her tresses in the way he knew drove her wild.

It was always like this with Hunter. This all-consuming need to hold on to each other so tightly, they'd never fall apart. Annie wrapped her legs around his waist and forced him deeper.

Hunter bent his head, bit her neck, leaving his mark. She cried out with pleasure, scratching his arms, drawing on his body as well. She'd make sure he never forgot her. Never forgot…

Panic consumed her once more, throwing her into action. She shoved at his chest, indicating she wanted him on his back. She followed him over, pounded herself up and down, up and down on his turgid flesh. Hunter's fingers gripped her hips, guiding her, pulling her toward him harder. Using his strength to drive her.

"Fuck," Hunter muttered. "More."

He sat up, pulling her off his cock. With strong, sure hands, he pushed her facedown over his mattress as he knelt behind her. Then he was there, inside her again, thrusting so deeply she feared they'd break the bed.

Annie took his pummeling blows, increasing the impact by meeting him halfway. Still it wasn't enough. She crawled forward slightly, flipping to her back once more. Hunter upped the ante, standing then dragging her body until her ass hovered at the edge of the mattress. She wrapped her ankles around his neck and Hunter accepted the invitation. He drove into her hard and she bit her lip to keep from screaming.

If anyone else was already awake, there was no way they wouldn't know what was going on in Hunter's bedroom. Typically, they kept their lovemaking in the house quieter, calmer, only indulging in the loud, kinky stuff while way out of earshot of other people.

So much for discretion.

Hunter grabbed one of her breasts and squeezed the ultra-sensitive flesh. She groaned, her fingers fisting in the sheets.

"More!" she demanded.

Hunter's gaze darkened as he quickened his pace. Twice he pinched her nipple, causing her to buck beneath him, her back arching on the bed. Then he rubbed her clit and her control was utterly destroyed. The white-hot lights of her orgasm blinded her. It was only here in this moment that the real world disappeared and her anxieties subsided.

Oh how she wished she could call this perfect place home.

Hunter slowly lowered her legs until her feet hit the floor. It was only then she realized he hadn't come.

She opened her eyes, her gaze eating up his handsome face, his muscular chest, the light sprinkling of hair that adorned it. "Hunter?"

He looked away from her, toward the nightstand. Opening the drawer, he pulled out a tube of lubrication. Though he'd promised to take her ass, he hadn't breached her with anything more than his finger.

"Say no, Annie, and this goes away. I won't do anything you don't want."

"I want it." The words fell from her lips without a second thought. She wanted every part of Hunter she could get. Wanted to create a thousand memories of him so she could take them out later, on the lonely nights, and remember.

"Roll over."

She turned easily, catching a second wind, her heart

starting to race. What he was about to do seemed wicked, like something they should only attempt during the darkest hour of night. Not now, when the bright morning sunshine was just starting to flood the room.

She jerked slightly when he drizzled some of the cool lube on her ass. Annie struggled to breathe as he slowly worked the gel inside, first with one finger, then—holy shit—with two.

"You're holding your breath."

"I am?"

He froze. "Should I stop?"

"Good God, no. I didn't realize how sensitive that area was."

He began thrusting shallowly, working slowly to stretch her. Neither of them spoke for several minutes as Annie acclimated herself to this new experience. Hunter's thoroughness and care as he prepared her to take him touched her heart. As if he hadn't already claimed enough of it, he was stealing yet another piece with his concern. He would never hurt her, never intentionally bring her pain.

Finally, his fingers disappeared. She glanced over her shoulder and saw that he'd donned a condom. He carefully coated it with lube as well.

"Ready?"

She nodded once, nudging her ass higher, inviting him in.

Hunter wiped the lube off his fingers with his sheet, giving her a mischievous grin. "Guess I'll be doing the laundry later."

She was amazed at his ability to provoke so many emotions inside her at once—happiness and horniness mingled together into one giant blob of bliss. The head of his cock nudged at her tight opening and she sucked in a deep breath.

"Don't do that," he cautioned. "Release that air slowly and push against my cock as I move in."

She followed his instructions, his cock slipping in an inch or so. Sweat rolled down Annie's brow.

Hunter reached around to rub her clit. She sighed at the pure ecstasy that touch produced and his cock slid in even farther. Hunter continued to play with her sexual hot buttons, stroking her clit, sucking on the back of her neck, pinching her nipples. Every teasing touch caused her body to relax more until he was fully lodged inside her ass.

He pressed his chest against her back and kissed her ear. "Do you like this?"

She nodded. "More than you'll ever know."

"My girl," he whispered. The words warmed her heart. What would she give to be his girl forever?

Before she could consider that answer, Hunter retreated a few inches, returning faster this time. The rhythm took her breath away. The first few thrusts pinched as she tried to decide whether the discomfort was a bit too close to true pain to be pleasurable. Before she could cry halt, though, her body gave way to the sensations, accepting them. Her pussy clenched the emptiness and she suddenly wished she had her vibrator.

Next time.

Please let there be a next time.

Hunter pumped into her solidly, though with less strength than he'd just taken her pussy. He was being careful, trying not to hurt her. She smiled—then pushed the envelope.

She met his thrusts, adding her own force to the cadence. Within moments, she heard the telltale signs of Hunter's impending climax. His breathing quickened, his fingers tightened as he pulled her hips toward him.

"God, Annie. Jesus. Fuck!"

She loved his mindless curses, loved the way his body jerked against hers when his orgasm overtook him. She felt each pulse as he erupted, filling the condom.

Exhaustion gave way. He pulled out slowly, as both of them slumped facedown on the bed. She didn't move for several minutes, too afraid to break the spell.

Hunter was quiet for so long she'd thought he'd fallen asleep. Then his eyelids lifted and he captured her gaze.

"I love you."

His words, spoken softly, penetrated every dark, lonely spot inside her.

"I love you too."

"Annie, I want—"

Before he could finish, a loud knock came at the door.

"Hey, brother," Dylan called through the wood. "Hate to interrupt, but we just got a call. There's some fancy-arse private jet about to touch down on our landing strip. Pilot says he's got Annie's dad onboard."

"Shit." Annie sat up rapidly, grabbing on to Hunter as a wave of light-headedness came over her. Her father? Here? In Oz?

Hunter, ever calm, cool and collected, yelled, "We'll be out in a minute."

"Okay."

Annie listened as Dylan's footsteps retreated, trying to figure out what the hell her father was doing here.

"Why would he come here?" she asked, more to herself than to Hunter.

"Do you think he could be worried about you?"

She scoffed. "Um, no."

Hunter frowned. "Why the bloody hell not? If my daughter took off halfway around the world to hook up with some bloke she'd met online without telling me, you can be damn sure I'd be on a plane, flying off to find her. I'd probably be tempted to beat her backside for it too."

"My dad's not like that."

"How do you know, Annie? I sort of get the impression you've never really tested him. From the stories you've told me, you've always walked the straight and narrow, getting good grades in school, earning that Magna Come thing, settling down near him in New York in an apartment he picked because he knew it was safe. Have you even done a single reckless thing in your life before this trip?"

"I don't consider this trip reckless." It was an inane answer and Hunter's face revealed his frustration.

"Well, you're the only one, besides maybe Dylan. I can tell you right now if you ever tried something so dangerous again, I'd be on the private jet *with* your dad and it wouldn't be a race to see who'd beat your arse first. I'd win."

Annie giggled. She knew he wasn't trying to be humorous, but there was something strangely amusing about his caveman posturing.

"What's so funny?"

"I'm waiting for you to start beating your chest, saying, 'me Tarzan, you Jane'."

Hunter dragged his hand through his hair and gave a frustrated sigh. "Bloody hell. I sound like a right fucking wanker, don't I? You're driving me nuts here, Annie. Every fucking day takes me one step closer to losing you. It's like there's a grenade in my gut and the pin's been drawn."

It was a perfect description. She felt exactly the same. She wanted to tell him that, but there wasn't time to say everything she needed to say. "I suppose we should get dressed and go meet my dad."

He rubbed his face wearily, clearly not happy with her response. "Fine. Let's go."

They managed to dress and make themselves look mildly decent in less than ten minutes. Annie had tried to cover up the hickey on her neck with makeup and she could spot four jagged scratches peeking out beneath the right sleeve of Hunter's t-shirt. If Hunter was right about her father's reason for flying to Australia, the next few minutes could be rather tense.

Annie and Hunter shared the front seat of the ute, while Dylan and Mutt jumped in the truck bed, which solidified Annie's suspicions. Dylan was here in case his brother needed backup.

They parked next to the landing strip just as the door to the jet opened. Stairs were lowered and Annie watched her father descend looking like a million bucks. Or, in his case, a billion.

While they'd all had time to adjust to the fact Joe Prince was at Farpoint, none of them expected the second guest who stepped out of the plane.

"Jesus," Dylan muttered. "Monnie."

Hunter glanced at his brother. "Monet?"

Dylan didn't answer. Instead he walked toward the jet. And her.

Annie grinned. She wasn't sure what had compelled her best friend to make such a long journey, but she prayed it ended well for both of them. Given Dylan's silent reserve since returning to Australia, it was obvious the first goodbye had hurt.

Joe passed Dylan halfway across the field. Neither man acknowledged the other. Dylan only had eyes for Monet. And her dad…well, he only had eyes for…

Annie took a deep breath as he approached.

She raised her hand in an awkward wave. "Hi, Dad."

"Don't you 'Hi Dad' me, Annabel Louise Prince."

"Annabel?" Hunter's voice mumbled next to her.

She shot his a warning glance. "Don't even think about it."

"Who are *you*?" Her father directed his question to Hunter.

Hunter bristled at the hostility in her dad's tone then seemed to recall what had brought him here. Given his impassioned speech in the bedroom, it was clear Hunter was siding with her father on the topic of her ill-advised trip to Oz.

Hunter stuck out his hand. "Hunter Sullivan. My family owns Farpoint Creek cattle station."

Joe reluctantly accepted Hunter's handshake. "Joe Prince. I assume you're the jackass who invited my daughter to travel all the way to Australia."

Annie tried to restrain her grin. "Um, no, Dad." She pointed over her father's shoulder toward Dylan. "He's the jackass."

Joe turned to look at the man he'd ignored. Dylan and Monet were talking, their heads close together. There was no mistaking the intimacy of the moment.

"Him? But I thought he and Monet—"

"Dylan and I crossed wires. He wasn't inviting me to Australia. He'd actually planned to come visit me in New York. Our flights sort of overlapped and I ended up in Sydney while he was in America."

"Christ, Annie."

"Hunter was still at the airport. He'd dropped Dylan off for his flight. He brought me back here."

"Why didn't you turn around and come home?"

She gave him a guilty grin. "I sort of finagled my way into the vacation time by promising to write a four-part series on an Australian cattle station for the magazine. Hunter was nice enough to let me shadow him."

"Nice, huh?" Her father's gaze drifted to her neck and

she fought hard not to raise her hand to cover the red mark there. Then he looked at Hunter, studying his face long and hard.

Hunter didn't cower under her father's intimidating glance. Instead, he raised the stakes on the silent game they were playing. He reached to take her hand and squeezed it. "I'll go wait in the ute while you and your dad sort this out. Mr. Prince, you're welcome to stay at the homestead with Annie and me if you'd like."

He leaned in and placed a quick but extremely proprietary kiss on her cheek. He was making a statement. He and Annie may not have known each other two weeks ago, but they knew each other now.

Hunter turned and walked back to the truck.

"What the hell is going on here?"

Annie wished she knew the answer to that question. "I could ask you the same question, Dad. Why are you here?"

"You missed Thanksgiving."

His response caught her off-guard and slightly irritated her. He knew she'd been upset about her sisters' plans for the holiday. "That's not a problem. I'll just catch a repeat of it on E sometime." It was a catty response she regretted the moment it left her lips. "Dad. I'm sorry. I—"

"No, Annie. You're right. We sort of made a mockery of the tradition, didn't we? Inviting in the cameras. Adding a bit of arguing to ramp up the drama."

"You argued?" For all her family's faults, they actually got along pretty well. While her sisters annoyed her with their exploits, they generally respected her desire to remain out of the limelight. True fights between them were few and far between.

Her dad's face suddenly looked sheepish. "The director said it would make the episode more interesting. Once we got rolling, we got a bit carried away."

"What did you argue about?"

"You."

She blinked, certain she'd heard him wrong. "Me?"

"Your sisters pretended to be upset about you missing the holiday. I defended you and it got out of hand. Cindy accused me of playing favorites, while Julia started insisting I loved you more than them."

Annie snorted. "Wow. Lots of acting going on then."

Her dad frowned. "That's the problem, Annie. It *stopped* being an act. A lot of things were said and…well, I was forced to admit some of your sisters' accusations were true."

"True?" Annie felt as if she'd suddenly stepped into quicksand and was engulfed up to her neck. Her chest felt tight. "They're the ones who've embraced the life you've provided for us. I'm the one who's always ungrateful, right?"

Her dad reached out and took her hand. "There isn't an ungrateful bone in your body. Dammit, Annie, how could you think such a thing?"

"You were so upset when I turned down your gift at graduation."

"I wasn't upset with *you*. I was mad at *myself*. I'd diminished all your hard work, dismissed it with some stupid grand gesture that was meaningless."

Annie shook her head. "It wasn't meaningless. It was thoughtful." She recalled Hunter's comment about it being sentimental. "*The Bulletin* meant a lot to you. I should have realized that and appreciated how precious the gift was."

"You're so much like your mother. I should have known better than to try to buy your affection like that."

Her father's admission caught her by surprise. "You don't have to buy my love. I already love you."

Joe chuckled. "And I'm a foolish man for failing to

realize it. I love you too, Annie. Very much. So tell me, why are you in Australia and who is this Hunter to you?"

She sighed. "I came here because I needed a break from my life. Then I realized I haven't been *living* a life. Not in a very long time. Hunter opened my eyes to that."

"You're in love with him."

She didn't bother to deny it. "Yes. I am."

Her father sighed heavily. "So much like your mother."

There was no anger in his statement. Instead it sounded like he was pleased, happy for her. She felt like she should point out the obvious obstacle. "He lives in Australia, Dad. I live in New York."

"That's just geography."

When he didn't elaborate, she narrowed her eyes. "That's it? Your only pearl of wisdom? What good is that to me? I need an answer, Dad."

Joe wrapped his arms around her and Annie tried to recall the last time her father had hugged her. It had been years. "Annabel Louise Prince. You've followed your own path since the day you first learned to walk. You've made your own decisions, taking turns I wouldn't have chosen for you. You don't need *me* to tell you what to do. You only need to listen to this." He tapped her chest, directly above her heart. "It's never steered you wrong before."

This time, *she* initiated the hug. He was right. This decision would be hers.

They parted and shared a smile. "And now, I think there's a young man over there in that godforsaken piece of shit truck waiting for you."

Annie laughed as she took her father's arm and they walked toward the ute together.

"Everything okay?" Hunter asked.

Annie nodded, her emotions too close to the surface. She was afraid to open her mouth, terrified they'd all come tumbling out. While she'd made peace with her dad, her future with Hunter was still up in the air.

"Hey, Dylan," Hunter called.

Dylan and Monet were still standing near the jet. Dylan looked up.

"You two want a ride back to the house?"

Dylan shook his head. "No. We'll walk back."

Annie looked at the two-seater truck before hopping into the bed, enjoying her father's look of surprise and Hunter's grin. She spent the trip back to the house lost in her own thoughts. She snuck a glance at Hunter. Her dad was right. She knew what she wanted.

Now all she had to do was hope Hunter he wanted the same.

AFTER A FEW STILTED words with Annie's father in the ute, Hunter dreaded what breakfast would be like. He should have known better than to waste the energy worrying about it.

Joe and Hazel chatted and laughed like long-lost friends. Hazel had managed to discover it wasn't Joe's first trip to Australia, which led to a lengthy discussion about the Sydney Opera House. Annie remained quiet throughout much of breakfast, only remarking with surprise and unconcealed disgust when her father picked up his Vegemite and toast, eating two slices with the genuine pleasure of a man who'd gone too long without a favorite treat. Joe didn't seem to share Annie's aversion to Vegemite.

After breakfast, Joe rose and offered to help Hazel with the dishes. Again, Hunter read the shock in Annie's features. He decided it was time for them to make a break for it. He excused himself and Annie as their parents began to clean up.

In the foyer, he grasped her hand. "Walk outside with me?"

She nodded. "Okay."

They walked in silence for a little while. Hunter didn't have a destination in mind until he spotted the little bench his mother had put near her garden. It was fairly secluded, the perfect place for them to talk.

They sat together as Hunter turned to face her.

"Annie—"

"Look, Hunter—"

They spoke simultaneously, both stopping abruptly.

"Sorry," Annie said. "Go ahead."

Hunter didn't bother with politeness. She offered. He took. "I want you to stay here."

"Stay here?"

"I know what you're going to say. You have a job and an apartment in New York. We've only known each other two weeks. Australia is too fucking hot. Your whole family lives in the States. I'm a thirty-year-old man living with his mother. There are a million reasons why this is a bloody idiotic request."

She laughed at his rambling speech. Better that, he decided, than running for the hills. "That's quite a list."

"Everything on it is true, but I'm still asking you to stay."

She glanced out at the garden and he struggled with her silence. Finally, she looked at him again. "Let me hear the other list."

He frowned. "What other list?"

"The reasons why I *should* stay."

He reached for her hand. "Because if you leave now, we'll never know what this could be. Because I can't stand

the thought of you sleeping so fucking far away from me."
He paused before giving her the most important reason.
"Because I love you."

She leaned closer, resting her forehead against his. "I
love you too."

"Does that mean you'll stay?"

She didn't answer right away. He watched the independent woman rear her head.

"What would I do? I studied to be a journalist. There
isn't much demand for those skills on the station. I can't
stay here indefinitely as a guest. I won't do that."

Hunter chuckled. Her response was so typically Annie.
Of course she didn't want to be a kept woman. Her father
had made that offer and she'd refused. She had far too
much pride and energy to stand idly by while everyone else
around her worked. "Do you need a job description? Jesus,
Annie. There are a thousand chores to be done around
here every day. How about we chisel out a few and make
them yours? They may not be fun or glamorous and I'm
worried you might get bored—"

"I'd never get bored here."

He sensed they were getting closer to an answer.
Hunter stroked her cheek softly. "Never is a long time."

"Have you ever gotten bored at Farpoint?"

He shook his head. "No, but—"

"But what?"

"This is my home."

She grinned. "I'm sort of hoping it might be mine
too."

He grasped her hands in his, kissing her knuckles. "It'll
be yours for however long you want to stay."

They moved in unison, neither of them able to resist,
sealing the deal with a kiss.

When they pulled apart, he marveled at the sheer joy

on her face. She lit up brighter than a Christmas tree. She was beautiful. She was staying.

She stood up and looked around at the hot desert he called home. "I have to admit, this is a nice twist."

"What do you mean?" he asked.

"The misplaced princess landed in Oz and realized she wasn't lost at all. She'd found home."

WANT *to know what happens to Dylan? Check out Claiming Her Cowboy, available now. Then read the entire Crossed Wires series. All four books are available now.*
Taming His Princess
Claiming Her Cowboy
Finding Her Master
Sharing Their Lover

Virginia native Mari Carr is a New York Times and USA TODAY bestseller of contemporary erotic romance novels. With over one million copies of her books sold, Mari was the winner of the Romance Writers of America's Passionate Plume award for her novella, Erotic Research. She has over a hundred published works, including her popular Wild Irish and Compass books, along with the Trinity Masters series she writes with Lila Dubois.

Subscribe to Mari's Newsletter

Lexxie Couper started writing when she was six and hasn't stopped since. She's not a deviant, but she does have a deviant's imagination and a desire to entertain readers with her words. Add the two together and you get romances that can make you laugh, cry, shake with fear or tremble with desire. Sometimes all at once. When she's not submerged in the worlds she creates, Lexxie's life revolves around her family, a husband who thinks she's insane, an indoor cat who likes to stalk shadows, and her daughters, who both utterly captured her heart and changed her life forever.

Contact Lexxie at lexxie@lexxiecouper.com, follow her on Twitter twitter.com/lexxie_couper or visit her at www.lexxiecouper.com where she occasionally makes a fool of herself on her blog.